SOME NEED NOT DIE

The Cost of Living

DANIEL HUNTINGTON

Soul Attitude Press

Cover photo: Photo by Sasha Freemind on Unsplash

Published by Soul Attitude Press
Pinellas Park, FL
www.soulattitudepress.com

ISBN 978-1-946338-65-5 (print)

ISBN 978-1-946338-66-2 (Kindle)

Printed in the United States of America
FIRST PRINTING

Dedication

I dedicate this book to my lovely wife of thirty years, Susan, who typed every word including several rewrites. Without her painstaking work and encouragement, this project would not have come to fruition.

Acknowledgments

I wish to thank my dear friend, Berkley Badger, author of *38 Hours ... the Faith of God*, for his valuable help and editing.

I also thank my good friends Joyce and Dale Vagts for their advice and suggestions.

Prologue

Frank felt a wave of panic surge through him. He found himself gripping the arms of the uncomfortable chair in the doctor's waiting room. The doctor's facial expression said it all. Jason was in trouble. Frank knew it before Dr. Burns uttered a word. "There's no easy way to say this, and I'm so sorry. There's nothing more we can do short of a transplant. Jason's heart is beyond repair."

"No," Frank's wife cried, sobbing. "It won't work. I've read everything I could find on the internet. The average wait for a donor heart is eight months. Over a hundred people on the list die each day while waiting. God, there must be something; there must be ... He's only nineteen years old." They sat speechless for a moment trying to come to grips with this devastating news.

Dr. Burns broke the silence. "There is another option," he said, "a very expensive option."

"Doc!" Frank shot back. "I own Gordon Technologies. I don't give a damn about the money. I'll write a check right now."

"No need for that. I am not involved with this medical group. But I do have a name and a number. If you're interested, I'll have them contact you."

In unison, Frank and his wife answered, "Yes."

As they stood up to leave, Frank said, "Thank you. Thank you. We'll keep in touch."

***

Frank wiped the sweat from his palms, rubbing his hands on his knees. He leaned back in the leather chair behind his dark mahogany desk and glanced out the window of his study, scarcely noting the shelves of rare books, the Oriental carpets, or the crystal decanter on the wet bar. His lush surroundings were so familiar, so expected that he paid them no heed at all. He looked at the Rolex he wore on his left wrist. The blue veins, liver spots, and pallid white skin of his hand disgusted him, made him feel every bit his seventy years. Gone were his toned muscles; his flashing green eyes, now dull with cataracts, were saddled with the sagging skin of a life lived in sheer decadence.

Frank glanced at his cell phone on the first ring. The screen read "unknown caller."

"Hello. This is Frank Gordon."

"Mr. Gordon, I'm calling with information concerning your son, Jason."

"Yes, yes. I've been expecting your call. What's the next step?"

"First we need to meet privately. Are you familiar with Bellaire Park?"

"Yes. It's not far from my home."

"In the parking area near the entrance of the jogging trail, I'll be in a silver Mercedes with a dealer tag. How about three thirty today?"

Frank hesitated. "None of this makes sense. I need some time to think."

"I understand," acknowledged the voice. "There's always the donor waiting list option."

"No. No," interrupted Frank. "I'll be there at three thirty today. I'm driving a gray Cadillac SUV."

"Fine. You'll be given complete instructions regarding financial requirements, and I'll fill you in on the remaining details."

Frank ended the call, put his cell back in his

hip pocket, and got up from his chair. He had four hours to kill before the meeting. He knew it would be hard, but he'd have to get his mind off what was happening. He picked up the morning paper and strolled out the back door toward the lake behind his house. Halfway around, he stopped and sat down on the green bench where he often read the daily news. His mind travelled back to Jason's childhood; things they did together, fishing, and little league. He relived the terror he felt that day Jason was leading the half-mile run at his school track meet when he collapsed and was rushed to the hospital, ending his athletic career.

Glancing at his watch, he noticed it was time to leave. Frank walked the short distance to the house and made the twenty-minute drive to Bellaire Park.

***

Frank approached the silver Mercedes. The driver lowered the window and motioned him into the passenger seat.

"Good afternoon, sir. I'm Vince."

"Vince who?"

"Vince is sufficient. As you must have already guessed, our services circumvent standard medical protocol. Therefore, names and locations are irrelevant. The main thing is to keep the main thing the main thing. And that, I'm sure you'll agree, is the life of your son, Jason."

"Yes, of course, of course," agreed Frank.

Frank was silent as Vince handed him a sealed envelope.

"Follow these instructions to the letter—no shortcuts and no deviations. When the funds are received, Jason will be taken to a state-of-the-art facility where the procedure will take place."

"May my wife and I accompany him?"

"I'm sorry, but no. However, while he is with us, he will be afforded periodic calls to home via a secure phone. I assure you he will be in excellent hands and will receive the best of care. That's the way it has to be. When Jason has sufficiently recovered, we will bring him home. Do you understand?"

"No," replied Frank. "But all I can do is leave it in God's hands."

***

Three weeks later, Jason was home working with his personal physical therapist. Frank stood with his arm around his wife's shoulder and remarked, "He looks like a million bucks . . . actually, more like three million. But that's the cost of living."

Chapter 1

It was commencement day at Davidson College. Five hundred students filed in and took their seats on the floor of the auditorium, while proud parents and family filled the seats, their cameras ready. Dean Sorenson approached the podium, prepared to give the welcoming address.

"Good morning, graduates, parents, and distinguished guests."

As the dean began his address, one student suddenly stood up with her fist raised and began to chant, "The school's unfair, and you don't care." She was followed by another and then another, until over forty students had taken up the chant. The protestors walked out following their leader, Rhonda Wells, the very popular student editor of the school paper.

Just when it seemed like order had been restored, another thirty or more students took up the chant and marched out of the building. Several hundred people outside joined the chant and several pounded on the doors, making it impossible to hear the speakers. Rhonda stood on a high mound, raising her arms up and down and encouraging the mob to get louder.

The noise and resulting chaos were so bad that the dean went forward without the planned speeches and motioned the remaining students to come forward one at a time, presenting their diploma while cameras flashed. The anger from both sides reached a fever pitch. Law enforcement dispersed the crowd outside, allowing the graduates and their families to leave.

Rhonda Wells's parents, Dr. Bruce Wells and his wife, Rita, left the auditorium devastated and embarrassed, apologizing to their many friends. They quickly walked to their car and made the two-hour drive home without meeting or speaking with their daughter.

The local affiliate of CNN covered the protest, and the reporter singled out Rhonda. "Why the demonstration? And who are you?"

"Rhonda Wells, and thanks for giving me the opportunity to speak. Davidson College has the worst record for admitting minority students and hiring minority professors. I have written articles in the school paper regarding this issue, but my words have fallen on deaf ears. It isn't fair; thus, the chant—the school's unfair, and they don't care." She was thrilled that the interview went national.

As a little girl, Rhonda had scorned her affluent lifestyle. She was the only child of Dr. Bruce Wells, a highly regarded cardiologist, and Rita Anderson Wells, who came from old New England money of the Anderson Ship Builder family. Rhonda would often give her possessions to other children in school—a sweater, her lunch money; once she even gave away a delicate gold bracelet given her by her grandmother. Rita contributed to Rhonda's penchant for causes. By the time she could walk, her mother would drag her from one volunteer project to another. From Trees for Brookline to Make a Wish Foundation to Habitat for Humanity, she was a veritable fountain of benevolent labor.

Rhonda craved the approval of her father but disagreed with him on virtually every social issue. He had hoped that she might one day follow him into the field of medicine, yet she chose journalism instead. Her father referred to the news media as *liberal whiners* who created rather than reported the news. "Always looking to tear things down, rather than build something," he would often rant. Or, "Bad news sells, so don't waste time on the positives," was another familiar complaint.

"Did you ever watch a skyscraper being built?" he would lecture Rhonda. "It requires hundreds of talented people—brilliant architects, skilled craftsmen, engineers, stonemasons, electricians, and designers. It takes years to create, but one uneducated jerk with a crane and a wrecking ball can tear it all down in a day. That wrecking ball is the news media."

As a teenager, Rhonda didn't understand how her father, a gifted heart surgeon who saved lives every day, would have such a seeming disregard for the average person. She developed a strong sensitivity for those who appeared helpless, with no voice. She demonstrated distain for the very rich, who she saw as unjust greedy bastards. She also had a low opinion of law enforcement, as she perceived them as inflicting brutality against the bottom rung of society. Rhonda developed a good-sized chip on her shoulder and displayed the tenacity of a pit bull. If there was a crusade to join, she jumped right in. This oftentimes resulted in an impassioned story under her name appearing in the college paper.

After the dust settled from the graduation protest, she packed her Spartan belongings, picked up her diploma from the dean's office, and then drove home to face her irate father.

As she drove up the winding tree-lined driveway to her home, she entered the four-car garage and parked her VW bug between her father's BMW and her mother's ES 400 Lexus. She caught her reflection in the window of her father's car. Her long curly blonde hair and her expressive green eyes and high cheekbones, along with her slim athletic body, gave her the appearance of an aristocrat, but she saw herself as a down-to-earth girl next door.

As was her custom, she entered the house through the connecting garage door and dropped her duffel bag in the adjoining laundry room.

"Anybody home?" she called out.

"In here," came her father's reply from his study.

Rhonda knew by his stern tone that he was not in a welcome-home mood; but she was not prepared for the onslaught that followed.

Dr. Wells laid aside the medical journal and stood up facing the door.

"Hi, Dad," she said, standing at the door of her dad's study. Leaning against the doorjamb, her hand shoved deep in the pockets of her khaki pants, she glanced down at her well-worn sweatshirt, a ratty-looking thing emblazoned with the slogan "stolen from Boston College," knowing it would irritate him. But at this point, she couldn't care less.

"Well . . . if it isn't Miss Hard Copy and *Inside Edition* all rolled into one."

"Nice to see you too," she replied, but her facial expression showed otherwise.

"Really, it is nice to see you, Rhonda. And I'm glad you're home. I just wish you would have left the attitude at school. Your mother and I were looking forward to seeing our only child graduate. Instead our only child turned out to be an embarrassment to the family by leading a ridiculous demonstration."

"What's so ridiculous about the truth?" Rhonda stated with furrowed brow as she locked eyes with her father.

"Nothing is wrong with the truth, if you're sure you have all the facts."

"So, you're saying I'm wrong?"

With a long sigh her father answered, "No. I'm saying it's the truth as you see it."

"Oh, I see. So I have to twist the truth until it fits your narrative?"

"No. What I'm saying is, until you've been there and done it, you can't see the big picture. At this point, you haven't even earned a paycheck or paid one dime in taxes. You need to contribute something before you start judging the world."

Rhonda walked to the small refrigerator in her father's study and grabbed a bottle of water. Removing the lid, she took a slow swallow. "Am I going to have to listen to the story about the architects and the wrecking ball again?"

"No!" His anger was showing, much against his will. "You don't have to listen to anything. You're a big shot with all the answers. You're the judge, the jury, and the executioner. You write about and criticize people you don't know or never took the time to get to know. You irresponsibly wrote their names in that rag you call a paper, accusing them of bigotry and prejudice."

"Well, Dad, I was given the editor's award from that rag, as you call it."

"Rhonda, I am not questioning your talent as an editor. What I'm saying is you never took the time to thoroughly investigate. Many of the people on that board are just as sensitive and concerned as you. And given time, they will right the wrongs. But they'll do it by working within the system, while you're more interested in tearing the system down."

"Dad, maybe the system is broken and needs to be torn down."

"Rhonda, this is personal for me. The people you've criticized and attacked have generously endowed the very institution that provided you your education and made you so damn smart. They are responsible for building the hospital where I practice and are personal friends. Perhaps you'd like to accompany me when I go ask them to dig a little deeper for the proposed pediatric wing."

"Are you finished?" she asked.

"Yes, I am, not that you heard a thing I've said or give a damn!"

Rhonda said nothing for a few minutes but stood with arms folded, looking out the large picture window. Only after her tension subsided did she speak.

"Dad, I'm sorry I insulted your friends. That was not my intention. And as far as paying dues and taxes, I'll be doing both beginning next week. I've taken a job in New York with a small but growing publication, *The City Voice*. Also, so not to embarrass you or your friends, I'll be writing under the pen name, Rhonda Rhodes, as an intern working under the tutelage of the highly respected columnist Phillip Brown."

"New York. Why New York? Why not something local?"

"Everyone knows New York is where the opportunities are."

"What about Todd? You two have been dating for a couple of years now. How does he feel about you moving to New York?"

"Todd has accepted a job as a tennis pro in Florida. So, regardless, it looks like a long-distance relationship at this point," she acknowledged with a little chink in her armor beginning to show. "I'm keeping his cat for him because he's not allowed pets in his building. We'll keep in touch via text like we do anyway. Who knows?" She sighed.

"Well," he admitted, "you're going to do what you believe is best. You always do. Your mother and I never tried to stifle your freedom or creativity. But remember—with freedom comes responsibility," he pointed out with less authority.

"I'll try to remember that. I really will." Her sarcasm was also waning. "I have a million things to do before I leave for New York. Is there anything else?"

"Yes, yes there is."

"What is it, Dad?"

"Your dad could really use a hug about now."

As they hugged, he said, "Honey, it's too bad that we are like oil and water, but I love you."

With that she said, "Love you too, Dad. I'll see you in the morning."

Later that night, Rhonda lay on her bed staring at the ceiling, unable to sleep. *God*, she thought. *I wish Dad and I could be on the same page just for once.*

Chapter 2

The alarm went off at exactly 6:00 a.m. Garth Kruger silenced the clock and instinctively reached over to touch his wife, Susan. She wasn't there. Garth noticed a light under the bedroom door and realized she was up and about. Garth showered, shaved, and dressed in his captain's uniform. He took one last look in the mirror; his fifty-four years were beginning to show. At six feet and weighing 205 pounds, his athletic physique was a testament to his high school years playing football and basketball and the pickup games he often played with his three brothers.

"Today, no matter what is going on, I'm going to squeeze out some time on my lunch hour to workout at the precinct gym," he told himself.

He fastened his NYPD chest shield, knotted his tie, and noticed that a haircut needed to be scheduled. Picking up his hat, he headed out of the bedroom and stopped as Susan met him with a steaming cup of coffee.

"Bacon and eggs almost ready, big guy."

He placed the coffee on the counter and gathered her in his arms, "I'd like my dessert first," he said as he kissed her tenderly.

Garth finished his breakfast, swallowed the last of his coffee, and stood to leave.

"Gotta go, Susie. I love you." He kissed her again and headed out the door.

Susan followed him and called out in her best *Hill Street Blues* impression, "Let's be careful out there."

Garth never tired of hearing it.

He backed out of the driveway and began to mentally formulate a plan that could lead to a massive drug bust. The notorious Leo Spanato controlled the lion's share of drug trade in his precinct. Garth's two undercover detectives on the case seemed very close to busting things wide open. The print and broadcast media had been relentlessly calling the precinct daily, seeking an update regarding his progress on the deaths of so many young people as a result of drug overdoses. Garth knew they were close and breaking up this drug ring would certainly get the press off his ass.

Turning right off the highway, the thought crossed his mind that just thinking about the press put him in a sour mood. According to his brother Paul, chief of police in Summerville, South Carolina, the small-town Southern press was fair and cooperative. His other brother, Kevin, didn't have this worry as a state trooper in Buffalo, New York. Kevin never talked to the press.

In fact, Garth, after graduating from City College and earning a degree in criminology, had considered joining his brother in Buffalo. But the pull of following in his father's footsteps was too strong. Garth instead enrolled in the New York City Police Academy, hoping to possibly work with his dad. Tragically, that dream never materialized. Just four months after Garth joined the force, his father was called to settle a domestic dispute. Subsequently, he was ambushed and died on the way to the hospital. From that day on, Garth was determined to be a dedicated police officer and a good loyal cop, just like his dad. *If only*, he reminisced, *Dad had lived to see me become captain of the Seventy-First Precinct.*

Garth pulled into his parking space in the underground garage. He entered the main room and took the time to greet and compliment the employees, from the highest-ranking officers to Ralph the custodian. As he walked into his private office, he spied the stack of files on his desk. His policy was, for the most part, open door. But if he intended to get through the stack, he would need some privacy. He closed the door and placed his hat on a side table before sitting down at his massive scarred oak desk.

He had begun separating files in order of urgency when Beth came on the intercom. "Captain, Sid Roth from the *Daily News* would like a moment."

Garth took a deep breath, slowly exhaled, and answered, "Okay, put him through. But I'd much prefer a root canal."

"Captain Kruger here."

"Yes, Captain. This is Sid Roth, *Daily News*. I'm calling to confirm a quote attributed to you regarding our homeless epidemic."

Garth sat back in his chair, looked at the ceiling, and rubbed his hands through his hair. "And what was the quote?"

"My source tells me that you said, and I quote, 'My precinct has far more challenges to deal with than a bunch of homeless people.' "

Garth now leaned forward and began to drum his fingers on his desk. "Mr. Roth, I'm going to say this real slow so you get it right. I never, ever made that remark. It must be very convenient to use the phrase *anonymous source*; therefore, you do not have to be accountable for what you print."

"I'm sorry you feel that way, Captain. I merely wanted to give you the opportunity to give your side of the story."

"I don't see it as having a particular side. I see it as reporting truth."

"Well, thank you for your time, Captain, and have a good day."

After Garth replaced the receiver, he looked at his watch, lamenting the time wasted, and turned back to his work. He made a mental note to read Roth's column in the morning.

***

As his day came to an end, Garth was relieved that his desk was completely void of files. He spent his last fifteen minutes briefing the night shift and left. On his way home, he formulated his agenda for this evening. Since the Rangers were playing the Black Hawks on TV and Chicago was in the central time zone, he reasoned that the game wouldn't start until eight thirty, giving him enough time for a quiet dinner at Susan's favorite restaurant, Bella Italian.

After they were seated by the hostess in a quiet corner of the restaurant, Garth ordered a merlot for himself and a Chablis for Susan. "Here's to us," he said, raising his glass.

They settled back, enjoying their wine, in no hurry to order.

Susan said, "Honey, do you remember the first time you brought me here when we were in college?"

"Do I remember? I was hoping that I had enough money to cover the bill."

Susan smiled saying, "I always wondered why you only ordered salad that night."

"Looking back, it was the best night of my life. I knew I was in love with you, but that night I was sure. We didn't waste much time after that night." He winked.

It was true. Six months later, they were married. And the following year, they were blessed with their daughter, Lisa.

Susan smiled warmly as they recalled together those early years. "Wasn't Lisa a beautiful baby?"

He answered, "Now she has grown into a beautiful woman, wife, and mother."

"I'm sorry, Garth. I know you wanted more children, but I guess God had other plans."

"Yes. But now we have a son-in-law and two wonderful grandchildren."

Susan replied, "I know you are a little disappointed that Ben is not interested in sports."

Garth paused and answered, "I guarantee you one thing, if grandpa has anything to do about it, Katie and Chipper will know the difference between a touchdown and a slap shot. I must admit, though, that it comes in handy to have a computer geek in the family."

The waiter served Susan her chicken marsala and Garth his fettuccine alfredo. They picked at their salad, enjoying their memories. Susan paused. She looked at Garth straight in his eyes, saying, "I love you and am so proud of your promotion to captain."

"Thank you, honey. You know I love being the captain of the Seventy-First Precinct. But it still stings that Wade Newman was appointed commissioner over me. Most of my colleagues agreed with me that Newman's work was less than professional. He was dishonest and not opposed to taking shortcuts and liberties. His disregard for details and stubborn attitude should have disqualified him. He wouldn't have lasted two weeks working under my father."

After the waiter cleared their dishes, Garth ordered a sambuca and a Baileys Irish Cream in lieu of dessert.

"Well, we both know that, after he married Jennifer, his rise to the office of commissioner was a given," Susan stated. They both knew that Newman's marriage to the daughter of Lieutenant Governor Gene Wilkins was the only reason Kruger hadn't gotten the job that should have rightfully been his.

Garth answered, "Everybody at the station was amazed at how his many reprimands were mysteriously deleted from his permanent record. It is what it is, but position and wealth can't replace peace and happiness. Speaking of happiness, the puck drops in twenty minutes. We need to be leaving."

They arrived home in time to hear the end of the national anthem. Garth thought, *It was a perfect evening—good wine and great company, culminating in the Rangers shutting out the Black Hawks. Life doesn't get any better than this.*

Chapter 3

Applicant number 1 arrived precisely at 7:00 p.m. At 7:05 p.m., applicant number 2 entered and took a seat in corresponding chair number 2. Fifty-five minutes later, eleven men had entered the room exactly on time—not a minute early or a minute late. As per strict instructions on their invitations, no one spoke or communicated in any way.

At eight o'clock, the room lights dimmed. A light came on behind a screen in front of the room, behind which the silhouette of a man appeared.

"Good evening," said their host in a pleasant, albeit electronically distorted voice. "You have been summoned here to continue the screening process. You have been selected from a core group of applicants numbering in the hundreds. Based on data from intellectual and psychological testing, you all come to us with excellent credentials and a great deal in common, which is, of course, by design."

"For example, you are all gifted physicians motivated by power and money. You all tend to be stoic and are men of few words. Also, you have all exhibited the ability to follow instructions to the letter. These are precisely the characteristics required. There is one other interesting thing that you all have in common . . . Every one of you has served time in prison."

The host paused briefly. "You all went to prison for a reason, and you served your sentence. Therefore, the subject shall never be broached again.

"Now, let me continue regarding the positions available. You will be employed to do surgery at a US government facility. The pay is three hundred thousand dollars per year. The government grant to fund this program extends for an undefined period of time.

"For the past three years, this program has been operating on a limited basis, utilizing only two surgeons. Now, we are ready to expand. Your retirement benefit for successfully completing your service shall be in excess of seven million dollars—tax-free."

The host waited several seconds and then

continued. "You should expect that you may lose some people; but for every person lost, countless lives will be saved. So, my friends, this is a noble undertaking; you must believe that, should you choose to join the group. This completes today's session.

"Please take a personal communication device from the table to your right. Each one has a number on it. Take the one with your assigned seat number. There is a reason for everything you are required to do. Keep the device on you twenty-four hours a day. It will not ring; it vibrates, so you must wear it constantly. You will be contacted in the near future. When a phone number appears on the device, call that number for further instructions.

"Please leave at two-minute intervals, beginning with number eleven and working backward.

"Tonight, you are to check into a hotel. Alone. You are not to have contact with anyone. Spend this evening thinking about what I've said. Think about the future—your future and the quality of life you will contribute to others and yourself. If not for them, then consider the money! Remember—always wear your device. It is waterproof. You will be contacted soon.

Good night."

As the light behind the screen faded and the room lights came on, the applicants left as instructed until the room was totally empty. The host knew all of its contents would be gone, as if no one had ever been there, as his team followed his instructions, scrubbing the room of any evidence of the meeting.

***

The host watched Dr. Rob Francis check into the Park Lane Hotel and cross the lobby, stopping to put his arm around an attractive young red head whom he recognized as socialite Jill Romano, wife of Mario Romano, a prominent, well-known lawyer. The two entered the elevator together, and the host noticed the elevator stopped on the fourth-floor concierge level. The host took the elevator to the same level and sat on a couch near the elevator.

Shortly thereafter, room service delivered a dinner tray and champagne to suite 4208, and Dr. Francis answered the door. Approximately two hours later, the couple left their room, took the elevator down to the lobby, and walked right by the host, who was sitting there. The host dialed Dr. Francis's communication device and watched him look at his wrist and kiss Jill goodbye. Without delay, Dr. Francis returned to his room and dialed the number.

After one ring, a voice said, "Hello, number three. Please take a cab to the boat launch at Dobbs Ferry. There will be a limo waiting for you. Get in without asking any questions. You will be given further instructions at rendezvous. Thank you." Click.

Dr. Francis paid the driver and stood there momentarily, letting his eyes adjust to the darkness. As the cab pulled away, he saw the headlights of the limo flash once. It was parked down near the river. As he approached the limo, the chauffer got out and opened the back door. Dr. Francis slid in next to a tall man, who smiled pleasantly.

"Hello," said the man. "I am your host. I spoke to the group earlier this evening." He extended his hand. "Dr. Francis, let me introduce myself. I am Jack Rollins."

"Pleased to meet you," Dr. Francis replied, shaking Jack's hand.

"Dr. Francis," Jack began, "as a surgeon specializing in organ transplants, you are well aware of the physical risks of the surgeries you perform and also the monetary rewards. We know that, before your little problem with the tax man, you were one of the most successful men in your field. Wouldn't it be nice to have a second chance?"

"Well, thank you, sir," Rob began. "But—"

"But," interrupted Jack, "you didn't even scratch the surface of your potential. Oh, it's not that you couldn't have tripled your cases; the problem was and is organ availability. As you know, over forty thousand Americans await donated organs, and fewer than half ever get them. The worldwide demand is double that, if not more. The elite group about to be born out of my team of surgeons will overcome the supply problem. Donors will be preapproved—blood type, tissue match, and complete DNA."

Jack reached out, helping himself to a bottle of water. "Would you like a water or, perhaps, a glass of wine?"

"Thank you. Merlot would be nice," Dr. Francis answered and relaxed, putting his arm on the back of the seat. "Jack, please call me Rob." He continued, "If I'm properly reading between the lines here, donors will have to come from our society and obviously against their will, not to mention very much against the law."

Jack leaned forward, positioning himself to

stare straight at Rob. "Let me ask you some-thing, Rob," Jack replied. "If you or I were to disappear tomorrow, what do you think would happen?"

"Well, I imagine that every law enforcement agency in the state and probably the FBI would spring into action. At least I would hope so," he said.

"Correct. But if you were a transient, nonpro-ductive, homeless vagrant, what do you sup-pose would happen?"

"I suppose there would be a bowl left over at the soup kitchen," he said with a cynical grin. "But a donor with a drug or alcohol addiction—"

Jack interrupted again, holding up his right hand in a stop gesture. "Not all homeless indi-gents are alcohol and drug users. Furthermore, a burned-out brain does not mean unhealthy kidneys. As you know, one can have a strong heart but a badly infected liver. The bottom line is this—monetarily speaking, it could be a bonanza! A human body is worth from $1.5 to $15 million depending upon how you slice it, no pun intended, based on the number of healthy organs and the wealth of the would-be recipient."

Rob removed his glasses and rubbed his eyes

for a moment, chewing on the stem. He sat back in the limo trying not to let his excitement show as he said, "Now I can see why the eleven of us in that room tonight will have a chance to retire young. One more question if I may, Jack. Will the harvest and implant procedures take place simultaneously in one facility?"

"Good question," Jack answered. "Our division is set up for harvest only. Charles here is director of logistics and delivery. His team will determine whether the recipient will come to us in advance of harvest; or, if time permits, we will ship organs by private jet to the required destination. Some procedures will be performed in hospitals that have household names, by physicians with the most respected credentials. All forms and documents will be perfectly reproduced. Do you have any more questions, doctor?"

"No. It seems you have covered everything."

"Not quite everything." Jack paused. "Well, there is one other matter. But first, I have to piss like a racehorse. C'mon, let's take a walk. Charles, come walk with us."

The three men strolled toward the river.

"It's a beautiful night, isn't it?" Rob addressed the comment to no one in particular.

"You know, doctor, near perfect compliance is not good enough. We must insist on 100 percent adherence to every detail."

"Of course, I understand," Rob said, nodding.

"Why then," asked Jack, "did you entertain a young woman in your suite when the instructions were to have no contact or communication at all? Period. That was just another test in this long process; such noncompliance cannot be tolerated."

"Surely, you are not considering rejecting my application for this small infraction," Rob argued with a nervous laugh. "It was just a dinner, some good wine, and some great sex. It's not the end of the world."

"Rob," Jack said as he turned and nodded to Charles, who was following two steps behind, "for you, I'm afraid it is."

Charles slowly raised the pistol equipped with a silencer, squeezing off one round to the back of Rob's head.

"Sir, what a waste," lamented Charles as the two men slid the body over the seawall.

"Yes, Charles," agreed the man who used the alias Jack Rollins. "What a waste indeed. There goes a small fortune down the river."

As the limo ride into the night continued,

Charles, in quiet introspection, spoke. "Sir, may I ask you a question?"

"Of course, Charles. What is it?"

"Well, sir," the puzzled chauffeur asked, "if applicant number three was slated for rejection, why did you take the time to explain all the details to him?"

Jack leaned back with his hands interwoven behind his head and stated, "Just practicing my speech, Charles . . . just practicing my speech."

Chapter 4

It was unseasonably cold for a spring night as Eddie Wheeler burrowed deep in the dumpster beneath the mountain of garbage-filled trash bags. He always marveled at the way his body heat remained within his cocoon of plastic can liners. He also knew the city crew would not arrive until at least seven in the morning. He drifted off, dreaming of summer afternoons and Little League Baseball games he'd played as a child with his dad as coach.

When Eddie was twelve, his father had been killed in a head-on collision by a drunk driver, and his life had changed forever. His mom had remarried, and Eddie had hated his step-father. By the time Eddie had reached the age of seventeen, his and his stepfather' truculent relationship had come to an abrupt end, and Eddie had been thrown out of his childhood home. The streets then had become his home.

At a quarter to six, as he climbed out of the dumpster, he came face-to-face with an NYPD cop.

"What's your name?" the cop barked.

"Wheeler, Eddie Wheeler."

As he was being loaded into a police van, he was told, "Sit tight, Wheeler, and keep your mouth shut."

Eddie offered no resistance; he knew resisting arrest could bring down the wrath of the boys in blue. He'd seen them in action before. Besides, being arrested for questioning was no big deal, and it may lead to a warm cell and a hot breakfast. The van was warm, and he dozed off and woke briefly as three more men were loaded into the vehicle. Eddie noticed one young black man sat shivering, hugging his knees, while his companion lay in the fetal position, retching uncontrollably. The third man, a middle-aged Hispanic, was bleeding from his nose. Eddie figured it was the result of either resisting the police or too much street-grade crack.

No one spoke even a word. Eddie, as did most street people, knew the Miranda: Anything you say can and will be held against you in a court of law.

The van had no windows, but judging by the speed, absence of stops, and the fact that it had been over an hour since he'd been picked up, it was obvious they were not going to the Seventy-First Precinct. Eddie had been arrested many times, and the precinct was his home away from the homeless. He chuckled at his own gallows humor.

After what seemed more than an hour, the van came to a stop. Eddie heard the rolling sound of an electronic gate. The van continued on, making two rights and a left before coming to a stop. The back door opened. They were greeted by what appeared to be medical personnel dressed in green hospital scrubs.

The sick youth, loaded onto a gurney, disappeared through a set of swinging double doors. The Hispanic, whose nosebleed had subsided, was led to a waiting wheelchair and taken through the same doors, followed by the young black man.

A few minutes later, Eddie was ushered away. He was directed down a brightly lit corridor with doors along each side twenty feet or so apart. It became apparent to Eddie that they had been dispatched in such a manner as to avoid their knowing the whereabouts of each other. Two-thirds of the way down the corridor, as they stopped, one of the attendants entered a code on the keypad next to the door.

As Eddie entered the room, a sick feeling in his stomach told him this was not your everyday holding cell, and he knew this was no ordinary arrest.

***

The week following graduation, Rhonda packed her car with four suitcases, along with Topspin, the cat, and headed for her new adventure in New York. The cost of housing in New York was outrageous to say the least. However, she had grown up in an equally outrageously wealthy family on both sides. Besides, in reality, she could enjoy a comfortable life on the generous trust fund left to her by her grandmother.

Rhonda was excited to find a small one-bedroom apartment in a middle-class neighborhood. She had fun furnishing it with what she referred to as "early poverty."

On Monday morning, she arrived at the office, excited to begin her new career. She was thrilled to be assigned an internship to senior columnist Phillip Brown, one of the most respected mentors in the business. He was always assigned the most promising up-and-coming interns. Rhonda's college awards, along with three published short stories, made her the odds-on favorite to be part of his elite team.

The two hit it off from the start. Rhonda found herself soaking up every word, idea, and technique Phillip offered, and Phillip was quick to admit that his young assistant was gifted beyond her years. She was focused on becoming a successful journalist and making a difference in the world. She thought to herself, *I will be the voice of those who have no voice, and I will do it by the power of the pen.*

The ten- to twelve-hour days literally flew by. She loved the excitement of working at a real newspaper.

Rhonda was sitting at her word processor thoroughly engrossed in a project assigned to her by Phillip when her phone rang.

She answered on the third ring and was still engrossed in her project when she recognized the hysterical voice of her mother.

"Rhonda, I don't know what to do."

"What is it, Mom? Tell me."

"It's your dad. Oh my God, I can't believe it."

"What about Dad?"

"He was at work and collapsed."

"Is he okay?"

"No, honey. He's gone, and I don't know what to do."

"Mom, I'm coming home. I'll be there as soon as possible. I'm leaving right now."

Rhonda rushed into Phillip's office, explaining her mom's call. "Phillip, I have to go right now. I'll fill you in on the details."

"Rhonda, I'm so sorry. If there's anything I can do, please call me at any hour."

Rhonda drove home, having difficulty seeing through the tears streaming down her face. When she arrived at her apartment, she grabbed her suitcase and threw together whatever clothes she thought she would need. Her actions were erratic. She was having trouble focusing on what needed to be done. She suddenly remembered Topspin. She ran next door and asked Mrs. Swanson if she would look in on her cat until she returned.

The drive home seemed endless. She couldn't believe this was happening. Her eyes were red from crying, and she felt sick to her stomach. As she drove up the family driveway, she didn't take time to park in the garage. She rushed into her house to her mom.

The funeral was gut-wrenching for Rhonda. The receiving line of family and respected colleagues seemed endless. It was filled with survivors and their stories. One tearfully quipped, "Your dad was a wonderful man. If not for Dr. Wells, I would not be here today."

Dr. Carson, the hospital administrator, boasted to Rhonda, "Your father was the best. He was the most dedicated on our staff. It will be so difficult to find anyone to fill his shoes."

As she was leaving the church, she heard a familiar voice behind her. "I'm so sorry. I got here as soon as I could."

"Todd." She gasped and ran into his arms sobbing.

They said nothing for the longest time, embracing.

Todd was the first to speak. "I'm sorry that I couldn't get here sooner, and I have to leave early tomorrow to get back to work. I wanted to be here for you. I'm so sorry. Your dad was such a great guy."

Todd followed Rhonda home. After a short while, he felt he needed to give her mom time alone with her daughter.

"Rhonda, I'm going to leave now. I'll call you tomorrow from the airport. Let's plan a weekend in the near future when everything settles down. I've missed you."

"Thanks for coming, Todd. I've missed you too. It meant so much to me that you came."

She stood in the doorway and watched him drive away in his rental car.

After the rest of the family left, Rhonda went to check on her mom and found her sitting in her favorite chair looking through a picture album—twenty-five years of their family life unfolding page by page.

"Mom, is there anything you need before I turn in?"

"No, honey. I just want to sit here and relive the good times we've had together."

Rhonda found it impossible to sleep, with memories of her dad swirling in her mind. She recalled the day he'd brought her new bike home and had worn himself out running beside her until she pulled away from him, riding on her own.

Even then at that age, she thought, *my independence would not allow me to rely on training wheels.*

She relived the many camcorder videos her father loved to produce of piano and dance recitals, her winning a seventh-grade spelling bee, and high school soccer games. He had even shot a video of her valedictorian high school speech. Her dad had likely contributed to her independent attitude, as he'd encouraged her throughout her childhood. How sad, she lamented, that the joys of yesterday could be blotted out and replaced by the political and social issues of adulthood.

As she drove back to New York, her thoughts returned to their last conversation. There were so many things she wished she had told him. She wished she had expressed to him how much she appreciated and truly loved him. There were so many words she longed to take back. Of this, she was certain: For years to come, she would have to just live with the "what-ifs" and "if onlys." She vowed, while driving on that stretch of highway, to do something meaningful with her life, as if that would balance the scale—something that would have made her father proud.

***

Returning back to work, Rhonda entered her small cubicle. The first thing she saw was a bronze nameplate on her desk. It said, "Rhonda Rhodes, Journalist." She picked it up and hugged it like a little girl who had just gotten a new doll. She turned and headed to Phillip's office.

"Phillip, you did this, didn't you?"

"No, Rhonda, you did it. You've earned the title," he said and smiled at her. He stood up and walked around his desk, clutching both her hands in his. With genuine sympathy, he said, "I'm so very sorry about your father. I cannot imagine how you must feel. I can't remember my dad, since he died of cancer when I was barely out of diapers."

"Thanks, Phillip. He was a good man, and I'll miss him. I'm trying to carry on, knowing my dad would be the first to say, 'Rhonda, get back to work. Life must go on.'"

"Sounds like a wise man," Phillip acknowledged. "If I can do anything, anything at all, please don't hesitate to ask. This is a family-first company. And you, Rhonda, are part of our family."

"I appreciate that, Phillip, but my best therapy will be getting back into my work."

He motioned for her to have a seat. "By the way, I'm glad you're here. The editor asked me to submit a review of your progress, and I wanted to share it with you first."

"Let's hear it," she said.

Opening her file, Phillip began, "Rhonda exhibits attributes of a first-rate journalist. Her tenacity when it comes to getting to the heart of a story is unequalled. That, along with her ability to make a story come alive, is exceedingly rare at this stage of her career. She is a natural wordsmith and writes with a style to which the readers can personally relate." After several additional comments he finished with, "She is a pleasure to work with. I see a bright future for her and a long tenure with the *City Voice*."

Rhonda thanked him for the kind words and left, feeling pretty good about herself. With so much sad news, she needed his encouraging words.

The following weeks, she immersed herself in her work. Phillip would begin each day with what he referred to as a creative session. He made her feel like part of the team, rather than an intern. They were very like-minded and had mutual respect for each other. When she was feeling down, he often encouraged her with remarks such as, "Tough times don't last, Rhonda, but tough people do." Phillip was fast becoming a much-needed father figure as well as a friend.

Their relationship morphed into a collaborative partnership. Everything was a joint project. The vision was to put their fledging paper on par with the big guys. Their current goal was to expose the city and state's total disregard for the thousands of homeless citizens.

They double-checked every detail of "Operation Taking It to the Streets." The project was approved by their editor. Their real work was about to begin. After a long day, Rhonda left work and stopped at a Burger King on the way home, buying a whopper and fries for herself and a fish sandwich without a bun for Topspin.

Before retiring for the night, Rhonda flipped on the TV to check the local news. The first words she heard hit her like a sledgehammer.

It was breaking news. "We are saddened to report that noted columnist Phillip Brown was gunned down tonight while talking to one of his unnamed sources. We will be right back after this break. Stay with us."

Rhonda was stunned, overwhelmed, and unable to organize her thoughts. *This can't be happening.* Her legs trembled; feeling faint, she sat down on the couch, taking several deep breaths.

No, no. This can't be happening. First my dad and now the best mentor I could ever hope for, gone from my life. God, tell me this isn't true.

Her thoughts were interrupted by her cell ringing. The caller ID identified the call was from Jim Stephens, senior editor.

"This is Rhonda."

"Have you seen the news?" he asked.

"Yes, sir. I'm sitting here trying to convince myself that it's all a terrible dream."

"Not a dream, Rhonda. More like our worst nightmare! We don't have all the facts and details. Perhaps he was getting too close to a major story. I know you must be in shock as we all are. But nevertheless, Phillip's favorite saying was, 'The show must go on.' I want to see you in my office first thing in the morning. It's very important that we talk."

"I'll be there, sir," she replied.

"It's getting late. Try and get some rest. Good night."

Rest, she thought. *There will be no rest tonight.*

Rhonda turned off the lights and walked into her bedroom. Topspin hopped onto her bed and sidled up to her as if he could feel her pain. Rhonda tossed and turned all night, sleeping very little.

The next morning, Rhonda made sure the cat had food, water, and a clean litter box before heading to the office. She found her stunned coworkers struggling to maintain their composure upon hearing the unimaginable news about their beloved friend and colleague. His positive attitude and jovial personality had kept the office atmosphere upbeat. He would be truly missed.

As she approached Jim Stephens's office, she saw him massaging his graying temples like someone nursing a migraine. The sadness on his face brought to mind an ancient quote: "The eyes are the windows of the soul." She knocked softly. He waved her in and motioned for her to have a seat.

"Good morning, sir," she said. "How are you holding up?"

"The only word I can think of is *numb*."

"I understand you and Phillip were fraternity brothers."

"Yes, Sig Phi Eps. But we were more like family. I expect to see him ambling in here any minute and hear one of his many Phillip-isms. In college, he was referred to as the court jester."

"I know what you mean, sir. He had a great sense of humor. But when it came time for business, he was focused."

"Speaking of being focused, Rhonda, there is a reason I needed you in here today. Phil was super enthusiastic about the project you and he have been working on regarding the city's homeless community. He was adamant that you play a leading role. He said it was your brainchild."

"Yes, sir, the idea came to me in college. My dream is to be the voice of the least and of the lost."

"This is my dilemma," said Jim. "Common sense tells me that a project of this magnitude and sensitivity could overwhelm most rookie reporters. But on the other hand, rookie or not, Phil saw you as our next star reporter."

"Wow," was all Rhonda could say. Even she, Miss Independence, was somewhat embarrassed by the compliment.

Jim leaned forward, looking into her eyes, and said, "Rhonda, can you do this?"

"Oh my God," she said. "If you give me this project, you will never regret it. I will do everything in my power to honor the memory of our friend Phillip. I promise."

Rhonda could not believe her ears when she heard him say, "This is against all standard operating procedure. But my gut says"—he paused momentarily—"Phil is right on this one. So go for it."

Rhonda was stoked! Her passion for this project went to the very core of her soul. Since her editor had given her the go-ahead, she couldn't wait to get started. She would be going undercover to write a series of articles on the plight of the homeless, up close and very personal.

An hour later, she was back home in her apartment, having left early to prepare for the following day. She was so excited she was practically bouncing around her apartment as she laid out the clothes she'd purchased at the thrift store—a worn white turtleneck shirt followed by a stained V-neck sweater and a camouflage jacket with a broken zipper. The weatherman called for cold temperatures, so she chose a pair of faded red sweatpants, crew socks, and well-worn tennis shoes. She topped it off with her dad's old Yankee baseball cap for good luck. She felt a combination of comfort and sadness as she looked at herself in the mirror wearing that baseball cap.

She was brought from her trance by Topspin as he did that wrap-around-the-ankle thing.

"You hungry?" she asked as she went to the fridge to get his tuna delight.

Her cell rang. It was her mom.

"Where have you been? This is the third time I've tried calling you today. I wish you would at least look at your texts once in a while."

"I'm sorry, Mom. I was in a meeting and had to silence my phone."

With a sigh, her mother answered, "I understand, Ronnie."

Rhonda smiled at the word *Ronnie*. Her father had called her that up to junior high, until Rhonda had begun to protest. There must be a psychological reason for her mother calling her that. Was she reverting back to when her dad was alive? Maybe this was her mother's way of dealing with the loss of her soul mate.

"Honey, the reason I called, I wondered if you could come home this weekend. You could take the shuttle to Logan. I could pick you up."

Rhonda walked over to the window and noticed the new buds beginning to come out on the oak tree. The noise from construction crew across the street drowned out her mother's voice, so she turned and walked into her room and sat on her bed.

"Mom, I'd love to. You don't know how much I miss you. But I have been given an assignment—not just any assignment, an awesome assignment."

"What kind of assignment calls for working through the weekend?"

"It's the nature of the profession I've chosen. Kind of like dad did his whole life. News and health emergencies are not limited to nine to five, Monday through Friday."

"You're right, honey. I guess I'm just lonely."

"It's okay. I understand. It's just that I'm so excited to get started. It's my very first investigative project on my own. I'm going undercover to write a series of articles on the homeless."

"Undercover? That sounds dangerous, honey."

"Mom, I'm not going to infiltrate the Mafia! I plan to expose the total disregard by the state and local government for the homeless people. The homeless people here in this area actually live and sleep on the streets; they have no help, no hope, and zero opportunity. It's a way of life we never experienced in our hometown. Many are physically and psychologically sick. Somebody needs to step up to help ... And I plan to be that *somebody*."

Rhonda became so passionate that she couldn't sit still any longer and began to pace around the bedroom. "We're timing the series to end the weekend of the annual Veterans Day Parade, which will be aired on television. We believe this will help create an awareness of all homeless, of which many are Veterans."

"Ronnie, I am happy for you, but please do be careful."

"Mom, I promise I won't take any unnecessary chances. When the assignment is over, I'll come home for an extralong weekend. I promise. I love you."

"I love you too, honey. You're all I have left. Bye."

"Bye, Mom."

Chapter 5

Rhonda stood watching the scene unfold. What a great opening for her first column.

To her right, a chauffeur opened the door to a stretch limo as four well-dressed men emerged, laughing at some unheard remark. Not fifteen feet away to her left, a young man was rummaging through a trash receptacle retrieving aluminum cans. There was something fundamentally wrong with this picture. Rhonda whispered some thoughts into her handheld tape recorder, which she always kept close by in her jacket pocket. *The money these men would spend for lunch today could sustain this person for a month*, she fumed to herself.

She cautiously approached him, as he appeared to be one of the city's homeless. "Excuse me, can you tell me what time it is?" Rhonda immediately realized what a stupid opening line it was.

The young man paused and looked at her like she was, indeed, stupid.

"Do I look like I got a watch?" he asked. "I'll just look at my new cell phone. How about that?! If I had a freakin' watch, I'd pawn it. Besides, you don't exactly look like you're goin' to some important meeting up town or nothin'," he said with sarcasm. "Why do people like you need to know what time it is anyway?"

"I just wanted to know. Do I need a reason?"

"Maybe you just wanted to talk to somebody is what I'm thinkin'."

Arms folded, leaning against a utility pole, she admitted, "Maybe."

"What's your name?" he asked.

"Rhonda."

"What's yours?"

"Pablo."

"Pablo who?"

"It don't make no difference. We don't need no last name on the streets. Rhonda, where you from?"

"Around. I've been on the streets since I was fifteen."

"Yeah, well I ain't never seen you around be-fore."

"It's a big city, and I keep moving. Besides I

keep to myself mostly," Rhonda answered.

"Where are you from?"

"I was born in Costa Rica, but that's a long sad story."

Looking at Rhonda intently, Pablo asked, "Have you had anything to eat today?"

"Yes, I had some fruit. The guy at the farmers market looked the other way," she lied. "I think he felt sorry for me. How about you? Have you eaten today?"

"Me? Yeah, I had danish and coffee at J-3 this morning."

"J-3. What's that?"

"John 3:16 Mission, Twenty-Fifth and Cedar. I spend a lot of time there."

"You think you could take me there?" Rhonda asked, sensing that the mission would be a reservoir of information.

Pablo said nothing.

"So, what do you think, could you take me there?"

"What do I think?" he echoed squinting at her. "I think you're fulla shit."

"What?!" snapped Rhonda, half-angered, half-shocked.

"You heard me. I think you're fulla shit."

"Well, you're entitled to your opinion."

"Look," he interrupted, "you say you've been on the street since you're fifteen years old. Right? So, you couldn't have graduated high school, right? Well, you talk real good English; you probably even went to college. I don't talk good English. But I know it when I hear it. Another thing, your fingernails are too clean, and your skin ain't seen no bad weather. You don't know about J-3. The dumbest bastard on the street knows about J-3. You say you keep to yourself, but you strike up a conversation with a stranger who's going through a garbage can."

Rhonda stood motionless, arms folded, leaning on every word Pablo was saying.

"Let me give you a clue, lady, 'cause you ain't got one. It takes more than worn-out clothes to be a, whatcha call it, a derelict. So, don't try to bullshit the bullshitter. And another thing, you say Joey at the farmers market looks the other way. That cheap bastard wouldn't give his own mother a piece of fruit if she was starving and had to turn tricks for her next meal. I don't know what your scam is, but I'm busy and in no mood to play your little game."

"Oh, you're too busy," Rhonda repeated, unable to resist. "Do you have an important meeting uptown?"

A faint smile appeared on Pablo's face; he tried to conceal it.

Jesus, she thought. *My first real project, and I blew my cover before lunchtime.*

"Okay, Pablo, you're right. I'm not homeless. I've never lived on the streets. But give me a chance to explain. Please."

He hesitated and looked at her with suspicion. "Okay, so explain."

"Look, this is a long story. Is there somewhere we can sit and talk?"

Pablo thought for a moment. "There's a place outside the library. They got tables where people sit and read on nice days."

There's plenty of foot traffic at a library, Rhonda assured herself. *I should be safe.* "That's great. Since I already blew my cover, what do you say I buy lunch if that's okay with you?"

"Suit yourself. But no more bullshit."

"Honest," conceded Rhonda as she raised her right hand as if being sworn in.

They walked together to a small deli just around the corner from the library called the Bagel Nosh, where she ordered two corned beef sandwiches and two drinks to go. Without talking, they sat eating their sandwiches while sitting at an old wooden picnic table behind the library. Rhonda observed Pablo's table manners. He used his napkin often—not her idea of a hungry street urchin. When he finished, he placed his sandwich wrapper in a trash receptacle, took a second look to fish out two aluminum cans, and then dropped his own Pepsi can into his plastic bag.

"I can't finish this, Pablo. Would you like the other half?"

"That would be great. Thank you," he said as he slipped the half-eaten sandwich into his jacket pocket.

"So," she asked, "where should we begin?"

"Let's begin with the truth—the whole truth and nothin' but the truth," Pablo stated with a smile. "And, by the way, thanks for the grub."

"You know, Pablo, you're very perceptive," she began.

Grinning, Pablo asked, "Is that good?"

"That's very good. It means you see through to the truth. You're nobody's fool, and it didn't take you long to see through me."

"Well, I think I know what you ain't, but I still don't know what you are."

"I am a journalist, an investigative reporter, doing a story on the homeless conditions in this area."

"Wait a minute. You telling me you get paid for writing stories about street people?"

"Yep, I get paid to cover all kinds of stories."

"So, why didn't you just come out and tell me? Why the Halloween costume and the bull-shit story?"

"Because I didn't think street people would trust a member of the establishment. I thought they might open up to one of their own."

"You got it backwards," Pablo snickered. "These bums don't trust nobody unless they can get something in return, and they know they can't get shit from each other."

"Do you mind if I get this on tape?" Rhonda asked pulling her mini tape recorder from her pocket.

"Okay by me, but it's pretty dumb carrying something like that. The scumbags around here been known to kill for a pair of tennis shoes, so don't be showing that thing around."

"I'm beginning to feel pretty stupid," Rhonda confessed.

"No, you're probably very smart, just not too street smart."

She thought about that for a moment and had to agree. "Could you help me become street smart?" she asked and then added, "For a fee of course!"

"A fee?"

"Yes. The paper has allotted me a nominal budget for consultants. You could be my eyes and ears on the street—my consultant."

"Let me get this straight. You mean you're gonna pay me to teach you how to be an uneducated, lazy street bum? Damn! I love this country more allatime."

"Would you introduce me to the people at J-3 for starters?"

Pablo stared at the ground in deep thought. "Ya know, they're always lookin' for bleedin' hearts to work for nothin'—ya know, volunteers."

Rhonda stared at Pablo and thought for a moment. "Yes, yes. I could volunteer. Pablo, you've helped me already. Could we meet tomorrow morning? There's a coffee shop about half a block south of where we were this morning. Say about nine o'clock?"

"They probably won't let me in, but let's give it a shot," he said. "Just don't you try to dress like a street person or not too fancy either."

As she prepared to leave, she got the feeling there was something more he wanted to say.

"Is there anything else?"

Pablo chose his words carefully. "I've been thinking. As long as we are going to be partners and all . . . maybe you can help me with something?"

"I will if I can."

"Well." He paused and thought for a moment, his mood becoming somber. "Like I said, I don't have much respect for some of the street people. Ya know, all street people are not equal, just like regular people. There's different kinds of people who live on the streets. Take me for instance. I'm homeless, but I'm not hopeless. I got a plan for the future. Anyways, my problem is this. I had a friend disappear a couple weeks ago, like right into thin air. My nose says something smells bad—something happened to him. We're kinda tight. He wouldn't just take off without saying somethin'. His name is Eddie, Eddie Wheeler."

"Have you gone to the police?" Rhonda asked.

"Yeah, right. I went over to the Seventy-First Precinct. They listen. They want last name and address, alla time lookin at me like I'm a turd. They tell me they'll keep an eye out and probably laughed their asses off when I went out the door—without them even writing a report. They figure a few less homeless, a few less problems."

"What can I do to help?" she asked with genuine concern.

"Well," he pointed out, "you talk good. You look pretty normal too. Maybe the captain at the precinct will listen to you. His name is Kruger. Maybe you can go and talk to him."

"Pablo, I promise I'll do what I can. We'll talk about it again tomorrow. But really I have to go now."

As she stood up to leave, Rhonda smiled and waved. "I'll see you tomorrow, Pablo."

"Gonzalez," he called back.

"Pardon me?"

"My last name . . . It's Gonzalez."

"Well then, I'll see you tomorrow, Mr. Gonzalez."

***

"Good morning, Mr. Wheeler," said the green-clad attendant. Eddie blinked several times, trying to focus. He vaguely remembered questions from the previous night. He also remembered an injection but nothing more.

As he absorbed his surroundings, he felt more bewilderment than fear. No iron bars, no obnoxious odor or screaming chaos associated with being arrested—this was not a cell. It was a room, a very nice room. He noticed the walls were painted a soft blue gray and decorated with colorful paintings. There was carpet on the floor, a couch, lamps, a flat-screen TV.

"Where am I?" he uttered.

"You are a guest of the state," answered the attendant in a reassuring voice, while continuing to explain. "There are two types of residents at this facility—guests and prisoners."

Eddie recognized this to be an orientation speech, so he listened carefully, allowing the man to continue.

"What you become is up to you. As a guest, this will be your quarters. Through that door"--he pointed--"is your private bath, complete with shower. In here"--he gestured--"is a kitchenette with a refrigerator and microwave, along with a TV monitor. You may order movies from this list," he explained, holding up a laminated card printed on both sides. "You will also select your meals from a daily menu. Snacks, juice, and soft drinks are available in your daily replenished fridge. Of course, your quarters will be locked at all times. However, you can summon an attendant when desired by pressing this button next to the TV. Before the attendant enters, he will instruct you via intercom to take a seat on your sofa, away from the door. Please do so immediately, as we can see you on the monitor from outside. Also, remain seated while the attendant is present.

"Mr. Wheeler, as a guest, your stay here will be a pleasant one as long as you follow the rules. If you break the rules, you will become a prisoner and will, without question, be transferred to a regular cell block. That is pretty much all I have for now. Do you have any questions?"

"Only a few for now," Eddie answered. "Why am I here? What did I do? And what am I charged with?"

"That is out of my department," answered the attendant. "But I can tell you this—a court-appointed attorney will visit you later today to explain the charges and assure you of your constitutional rights. I'm sure everything will be fine," he said with a smile. "Now I must go. If you need anything, please ring."

As the door closed, the sound of the dead bolt said he was still a prisoner.

***

Rhonda was sitting at her desk at the *City*

Voice deep in thought while tapping her pen on the desk. She hoped that her first article set the stage for subsequent stories on this subject. She sat critiquing her article from yesterday— "Plight of the Homeless" (part 1 of a series), the *City Voice*, Rhonda Rhodes, columnist:

I made a new friend yesterday. His name is Pablo. He is one of an estimated 63,000 homeless people living (if you can call it living) on the streets of our community. He listed some of the advantages of his lifestyle. No annoying phone calls at dinnertime from someone selling time-shares. "No phone . . . no calls," he joked. No property taxes, no junk mail. No pruning, trimming, or lawn mowing. These are some of the pleasantries of which he boasts.

This homeless person is pretty much like the rest of us. He has good days and bad days; he laughs, cries, and bleeds like everybody else. He will not panhandle. Nor will he work for food. But he will work for cash.

His only real gripe is being pigeonholed as a lazy, drunken drug addict who wants to live off the dole. He is quick to point out that thousands of homeless don't drink, panhandle, or take drugs. Many receive no government help at all. Some find a place to live. In fact, he points out, "I have a home. I just don't have a home address."

But what happens when the homeless need police protection? When fear is their constant companion—fear of being beaten up or, worse, killed for a warm coat or a pair of tennis shoes? They sleep with one eye open, hoping to get through the night unmolested. The NYPD, and specifically the Seventy-First Precinct seem to look the other way. When a homeless person is killed, mugged, or raped, how many man-hours do you suppose are allocated to finding the perpetrator? Their attitude—one less homeless, one less problem.

Pablo, for example, is convinced that something bad has happened to a friend of his, Eddie Wheeler. He personally visited the Seventy-First to file a missing person's report. Guess what their first question was? What is his last known address?

"I don't know," Pablo scoffed. "The Forty-Ninth Street dumpster behind the Chinese restaurant? Or maybe it was one of the large concrete pipes in the storage lot they call Culvert City. Phone numbers? Home and work?"

I'm not making this up folks. The bottom line is this—if you don't have an address, phone number, or a membership to the downtown athletic club, you don't get a great deal of attention from the boys in blue. No missing person report has been filed. No all-points bulletin was issued. "We'll keep our eyes open," one officer stoically promised. I assure you, we won't be seeing Eddie's picture on a milk carton anytime soon.

Garth Kruger, captain of the Seventy-First Precinct, was unavailable for comment. In the meantime, Pablo's friend Eddie is still unaccounted for. I wonder how long it would take New York's finest to locate Eddie if he voted on Election Day or made an annual contribution to the Policeman's Benevolent Association.

She laid the paper aside, satisfied that the important points were made and that it was interesting enough to capture the reader's attention and, hopefully, touch some hearts.

Her phone rang, and the receptionist announced that Captain Kruger was on line 3.

When Rhonda heard it was Kruger, she braced herself for a confrontation. She punched the button—determining not to be intimidated.

"This is Rhonda."

"Good morning, Ms. Rhodes," Garth responded.

Rhonda noticed he accentuated the z in Ms. She wondered if he was intentionally being condescending.

"I'm returning your call from yesterday afternoon."

"Oh yes, Captain. I was calling regarding a story that I'm covering."

"And how is the story coming along?" he asked.

"Well, uh, part one is finished, Captain. I wanted your input, but you didn't return my call. So, I had to go to press with it."

"But I am returning your call. You're my first call this morning," he declared.

"I wanted to talk to you yesterday before we went to press."

"I see. You had a deadline to meet?"

"Yes. You might say that."

"Have you been working on this story long?" He paused. "Ms. Rhodes?"

"May I ask where you're going with this line of questioning, Captain?" she asked, realizing that he was, indeed, being condescending.

"Well, Ms. Rhodes, it seems to me that, if you really wanted my input on the missing homeless situation, you might have given me more than eight minutes to get back with you."

At this point, Rhonda realized that he must have read her column.

"What do you mean eight minutes?"

"Your call came in at 4:52 p.m.; the shift change is at 5:00 p.m. I spend the last fifteen minutes each day briefing the next shift. I only got your message first thing this morning."

"Captain, I told the receptionist that you could call me up until 10:00 p.m."

"Did you tell her it was urgent?"

"Well, no, but—"

"Did you ask her to reach me on my cell?"

"No, I didn't, but I did leave an alternate number, as that's all I'm obligated to do."

"I'm sorry. I was under the impression that you are obligated to get the facts—all the facts!"

"Captain, your sarcasm is not necessary."

"Well, excuse me if I seem a little out of sorts, but my name, my reputation, and my precinct was blindsided by you and your paper. You know, Ms. Rhodes, when you wrote Captain Kruger was unavailable for comment, your readers might easily assume that I'm deliberately avoiding the situation. Do they teach that little trick in journalism school?"

"Trick? I resent the implication that I would—

"

"And I resent the way you handled the story. If you're honest with yourself, you will admit you've made a mistake." Garth paused a few seconds and continued. "This isn't the end of my career. I'll get over it. But in the future, I hope you will exercise a little basic professional courtesy."

"Captain, I'm sorry if you don't approve of my methods, but I don't intend to listen to a lecture. You're beginning to sound like my—"

"Like your what?"

"Never mind. It's not important. Goodbye," she said and hung up the phone.

At that moment, she didn't feel very tough. She hated the self-doubt and didn't feel like she'd won this particular round with Captain Kruger. This wasn't over.

Chapter 6

The phone was ringing as Garth entered his office. He took time to hang his jacket in a small closet in the corner before sinking into his large brown leather chair. After straightening several items on the huge oak desk, he fished a legal pad from the middle drawer. Only then did he quiet the incessant ringing from his desk phone.

"Captain Kruger," he answered in a pleasant voice.

"Where in the hell have you been hiding? I've been calling you all morning."

Garth could tell by the tone of Wade Newman's voice that he was pissed off, fully prepared, and intending to make Garth's day as miserable as possible.

"Good morning, sir," Garth replied in a mocking good-natured tone. Wade Newman was the last person he needed on his ass today. "Let's see, first I had breakfast with the mayor, and then I got a call from the president. And then—"

"Garth, goddamn it, this is serious, and I'm in no mood for your bullshit."

"Forgive me for being in a good mood, sir. I don't know what came over me," he quipped, rolling his eyes while making a sophomoric hand gesture one would expect from a teenager responding to a jerk-off friend. "What can I do for you?"

"The first thing you can do is explain to me the article in the *Daily News*, where you made insensitive remarks toward the homeless community."

"Commissioner, you know damn well that the press thrives on fake news obtained from unnamed sources. I did not make that comment. How else can I help you?"

"For starters, you might try to provide me with some answers. Spanato's making us all look like fucking Keystone Cops, and it's your responsibility to make something happen. Your precinct is a quagmire of drugs, and we all know Spanato and his boys are behind the cartel. The press is on my ass like flypaper looking for answers. What the fuck am I supposed to tell them?"

"Tell them to make something up. They will anyway."

"Oh, you're a regular fuckin' comedian this morning, but let me tell you something, Kruger. I'm not going to cover your ass much longer. I want some fuckin' answers, and I want them now."

"Look, I'm doing everything I can with what I've got. When we have something solid, you'll be the first to know. Now, sir, here's a little positive information for you. We have two undercover detectives, Cal Haley and Doug Brown, who are really close to getting inside. They're like pit bulls. They've been buying and selling for six months now. Anyway, they've been invited to a little shindig tonight. They'll be wired, and we will be one street over in a Mayflower van . . . We won't move in unless we have something to go on. One thing we do know."

"Yeah, what's that?"

"We ran a check on the address. The building is owned by one Mike Battaglia."

"So?"

"He's married to the former Anita Spanato, Leo's sister. I'll be there personally to direct the operation."

Newman, in his normal I'm-your-supervisor

voice, replied, "I certainly admire your dedication."

"Thank you for the compliment."   Garth couldn't hold back his smile. "It's nice to be appreciated."

"Another thing."

"Yes, sir?"

"I'll expect a report on my desk by noon tomorrow."

"Certainly, sir, and do have a great day." Garth laughed out loud as the commissioner slammed down the phone. He leaned back in his chair shaking his head thinking. *I should have fired that son of a bitch years ago when I had the opportunity.*

***

Rhonda parked her car across the street and scanned the crowd, looking for Pablo.

From behind her came his familiar voice. "Yo, Rhonda, ya got nice wheels! Yesterday you were homeless. Today, ya got your own car. You come a long way, baby," he teased.

"Well, it's a cheap car, not popular with thieves. Let's go in, have a bagel, and plan our day."

"Okay by me, boss," said Pablo as he held the

door open, following her into the coffee shop. "Ya know, I can't keep letting you pick up the tab. Even the homeless got some pride."

"Not to worry," Rhonda assured him. "The paper picks up reasonable expenses. Oh, by the way, before I forget, I received an advance on your fee." She pushed a check across the table. "It's a hundred dollars. I can get it cashed for you, if you like."

"Thanks, but that's okay. I'll deposit it later today."

Rhonda froze, the bagel halfway to her mouth, a bewildered look on her face.

"What?" asked Pablo. "Is it illegal for a homeless person to have a bank account?"

"No," she stammered. "Just a little unusual I would think."

"Well, I'm a pretty unusual guy."

Rhonda smiled, thinking, *So much for preconceived notions. Apparently, I still have more to learn.*

"I told you I had a plan," Pablo reminded her. "I'll tell you about it on the way to J-3."

As they crossed the street and got into her car, Rhonda insisted he buckle his seat belt.

"You know," Rhonda began as she maneuvered the car into traffic, "you are a very fascinating person. From a reporter's point of view, you're an excellent subject—very quotable and somewhat of a walking enigma."

"A walkin' what?" Pablo laughed.

"It means you're a mystery and not at all what you appear to be. You're homeless; you speak street jargon; but you're also neat, clean shaven; and of all things, you've got a bank account? You talk about a plan for the future. That's not something your everyday indigent would do."

"Turn right at the second light and another right on Cedar. J-3's four blocks down on the left." Pablo leaned back in his seat, seeming to enjoy the spotlight. "My plan," he announced, "is to own my own Buy Here Pay Here used car lot. You know, bad credit, no credit, everybody rides. I'm calling it, the Last-Chance Car Company, on accounta my customers can't get credit from nobody else."

"You are taking a big risk giving people a car without collateral," warned Rhonda.

"What do you mean?" Pablo replied. "I buy a car at auction for five hundred dollars, sell it for fifteen hundred with three hundred down and fifty dollars per week. If the guy keeps the car a month, I break even. If I need to repo the ride,

I start over with three hundred down. Now I'm ahead. Sometimes, you sell the same car three or four times. My company motto is gonna be 'The best way to get back on your feet is to miss a car payment.' This is J-3. Pull around back."

Rhonda stopped the car but sat with a look of deep concern on her face, saying nothing.

"Somethin' wrong?" asked Pablo.

"Something about your plan strikes me as very wrong. It's exploitive ... You plan to take advantage of poor people who have no credit and that is—"

"Whoa," he interrupted. "They got no credit, maybe bad credit, 'cause they stiffed the last guy they bought a car from. It's payback time. Besides, I'm given 'em a second chance. That's more than I've been given. They pay me, I give 'em a good credit rating."

"But you are gouging them on the price of the car in the first place," she countered.

"That's the price to pay to get good credit back." Pablo shrugged.

"What happens if one of your customers blows an engine? What kind of warranty will you offer?"

"Warranty?" chuckled Pablo. "If the customer drives off the lot and the car breaks in half, he gets to keep both halves. As long as I'm paid in full, what do I care?"

"Good God." Rhonda sighed as she stepped out of her car. "You're a homeless conservative capitalist!"

"Hey, that's got a nice ring to it."

As they exited the car, Rhonda noticed the run-down neighborhood. Grown men were pushing shopping carts loaded with what she assumed were all their meager belongings. Others were parking their bicycles before entering the mission. The building was in bad repair and could definitely use a paint job. There was a stench in the area where people obviously must relieve themselves.

"Welcome to J-3," Pablo said as he pointed the way to the front door. "It's time to meet John and Sarah.

"Sarah," Pablo announced, "I got you some free labor. This is my friend Rhonda."

"Praise Jesus," Sarah Barnes exclaimed as she clasped her hands together and looked toward the ceiling. "We have been so understaffed these last few months. I just knew the Lord would send us a volunteer!

"John," she shouted to her husband. "Come here and meet Rhonda. She has volunteered to help us with God's work."

John took Rhonda's hand in both of his and smiled. "Ask and thou shall receive. Our prayers have been answered."

"Well," said Rhonda, feeling a little overwhelmed by the reception. "I don't know what I can do, but I'm willing to help wherever I can."

"Oh my," gushed Sarah. "There is so much to be done. I don't know where to begin. You can drive the van or cook or help fill out job applications. You could take blood samples for HIV testing, or you could—"

"Whoa!" Rhonda laughed. "That's enough to keep me busy for a while! When do I start?"

John answered, "I just got a call from St. Jerome's. It seems they had a wedding reception—oodles of food left over, still refrigerated. Billy and Willy can go with you to help load the van."

"Billy and who?" she asked.

"Wilma. She's Billy's closest friend in the world. Saved him from an overdose," John explained. "We call her Willy. Poor thing has the mind of an eight-year-old child but is a loyal soul. Billy is only slightly better. At least he works like a plow horse. Sadly, his IQ is about the same."

"Suffer the little children to come unto me," quoted Sarah in a loving way toward her helpers.

"Amen," answered John.

Rhonda left Sarah's office with directions to St. Jerome and literally bumped into two of the strangest-looking characters she had ever seen. The man was approximately thirty-five years old. He stood five foot six inches tall and had four front teeth missing and mousy brown hair, obviously cut by his little companion. He wore green polyester plaid slacks, a faded NYU sweatshirt, and an old pair of high-top tennis shoes with no socks and laces he'd salvaged from a discarded pair of hiking boots.

" 'Scuse me," he said. "Mr. John said for us to go with you and help."

Rhonda hesitated momentarily. "Oh, you must be Billy."

"Yes, I am. And this is Willy. She my girlfren."

"How are you, Willy?" Rhonda asked in a warm, caring tone.

Willy giggled and covered her face with both hands as she shifted from one foot to the other. Her hair was dark brown like Billy's. She wore a tattered, gray flannel athletic sweat suit over a brown turtle neck sweater and brown rubber boots that came to her knees, into which her pant legs were tucked.

"She bashful," said Billy. "She love only me, and I love only her."

This brought more giggles from Willy.

"We had better get a move on," declared Rhonda as she led the way out the back door.

Willy and Billy followed, both with the same stooped forward, shuffling gait, Billy leading, with Willy in tow. Rhonda went to the driver's side of the van, got in, and started the engine. When Billy and Willy were in and the doors were closed, she pulled out of the parking spot. They exchanged small talk on the way to the reception hall and, once there, started loading the van.

***

In little more than an hour, the van was loaded with a variety of items, including hams, turkey breasts, and several blocks of cheese. *A pretty good haul*, thought Rhonda. *The people at the John 3:16 will eat well tonight.*

"Man do not live by bread alone," murmured Billy. "Miss Sarah and Mr. John tell everybody that."

After loading the last box, Rhonda closed the

van doors. Willy and Billy buckled their seat belts, and Rhonda started the drive back to the mission.

"How long have you known Miss Sarah and Mr. John?" inquired Rhonda.

"Oh, a long time. Me an' Willy, we help do the Lord's work. Miss Sarah pray for me an' Willy. She says Jesus love us."

From the back seat came a surprisingly beautiful voice. "Jesus loves me. This I know, for the Bible tells me so."

Billy joined in loudly, his voice very much off key. "Little ones to him belong."

By the time they arrived back at the mission, Rhonda, who only attended Sunday school sporadically as a child, knew all the words.

*****

Rhonda arrived promptly at the Seventy-First Precinct and slid her card across the receptionist's desk.

"Good morning," Rhonda said smiling. I have an appointment with Captain Kruger.

"Of course. He's expecting you," replied the receptionist. "Please follow me."

She was led down a long hall to a frosted glass door with the words "Precinct Captain" printed across the upper pane. The receptionist held the heavy door for her to enter, followed her in, and then handed Garth the card before turning to leave.

Captain Kruger's appearance wasn't anything like Rhonda had visualized. He had a warm smile, and absent was the beer belly most men his age had. He appeared younger and taller than she'd imagined. His office seemed homey, as it was decorated with many photos, one being a collage of four uniformed officers, one of which was Captain Kruger. His walls were adorned with several framed awards, including diplomas from New York City College and the New York City Police Academy. On another wall was a giant map of the city with various colored stickpins on it.

The captain stood as Rhonda entered and motioned her to take a seat in one of the chairs in front of his desk. She noticed the framed family photos on the credenza directly behind him.

"So, Miss Wells," Garth asked as he studied her business card, "how can I be of service to you and the *City Voice*?"

"Captain, when we last spoke, you had taken exception to the comments in my column regarding a homeless person who had gone missing."

"Actually, if my memory serves me, I took exception to your implying that my office was not taking the issue seriously."

"Captain Kruger, it was not my intention to question your professionalism."

"Well, it seems we are both guilty of false assumptions. So let's start over. What can I do for you today?"

Rhonda leaned forward and said, "I'm here on behalf of a friend."

"Oh, and who would that be?"

"His name is Pablo, Pablo Gonzalez. He's a homeless person."

"And why isn't Mr. Gonzalez here with you?"

"He has been here, but nobody would listen to him. So, he asked me to intercede. His friend Eddie Wheeler is missing. He disappeared without a trace—just gone!"

"Gone," he repeated. "Gone from where?"

"Gone from the streets. Gone from the face of the earth," Rhonda said tersely, her frustration beginning to show. "I don't know from where or to where, but it's the responsibility of the police department to investigate."

"Fine. Give me a name, last known address,

next of kin, or the name of some relative, and we'll do a missing persons check right away."

"Please don't try to placate me, Captain," she chided. "You know I can't give you house numbers of the homeless or last names or next of kin. You also know that the homeless are especially vulnerable to the absolute worst atrocities. But they don't pay taxes and they don't vote. Nor do they buy tickets to the policeman's ball. They have no power, no voice, and no rights. There are hundreds of Rodney Kings out there being whipped into shape by dozens of the Mark Fuhrman types. Let's not be coy! You know it, and I know it. Let me tell you something else, Captain. They do have a voice. If you don't believe me, read part two of my series in tomorrow's paper."

Hearing that, Garth just shook his head and smiled. He sat silently, his fingertips pressed lightly together as if in prayer. "Ms. Rhodes," he began, "first let me say that all cops are not like Mark Fuhrman. And I resent the implication.

"Another thing, do yourself a favor. Don't pull that pen-is-mightier-than-the-sword crap with me. I've heard it all before, and it's not going to help your cause. This may come as a shock to you, but you don't have to wear John

Lennon glasses and leg warmers to care about people—to be sensitive. I don't mean to lecture you. But of all people, you, a journalist, need to be objective. Objectivity is far more important than being politically correct."

"Are you finished?" Rhonda impatiently asked.

"No. I'm just beginning. I want to begin by explaining what I'm up against. You see, in order to assign men to a case, I need a shred of evidence that a crime has been committed. With the manpower at my disposal, I must prioritize and report to my superiors. We have limited resources.

"A murder in progress takes precedence over a dead body . . . a dead body over a suspected kidnapping . . . which takes precedence over jaywalking. I don't mean to be trite. But you can see where I'm coming from, can't you?"

"So, what do we do?" Rhonda asked with resignation. "Nothing?"

"No, we can do something. It's not much, but it's something."

"What is that, Captain?" she asked, her anger subsiding.

"I have undercover detectives on the streets posing as junkies. It's a drug operation, but I'll ask them to snoop around the missing person's angle. I can't make any promises, but it won't hurt to try."

As she stood to leave, Rhonda replied, "I appreciate anything you can do, Captain."

Garth stood up and offered his hand, which she accepted. She walked out of the building with a different opinion of Captain Kruger than the one she'd gone in with. He seemed honest and sincere, however blunt at times. He appeared to her as someone with strong convictions, rather than someone who would play word games. Rhonda left his office hoping that his detectives might come up with some evidence as to the location of Pablo's friend Eddie Wheeler.

***

Eddie Wheeler was sitting on his couch looking through a *National Geographic* magazine when he heard the click of the dead bolt.

"Please remain in your seat, Mr. Wheeler," came a voice on the intercom. "Your attorney is here to meet with you."

Eddie, as instructed, went to the sofa and sat down. The door opened, and in walked a man who appeared to be not over thirty. He was roughly five foot nine inches tall with coal-black, curly hair cut short all over except in the back, which dangled over his collar in a surfer cut style. He looked like the type who wore his baseball cap backwards.

"My name is Barry Hirsch," he announced as he pulled a straight back chair directly in front of Eddie while placing his attachÃ© case on his lap. "I will be your counsel. If for any reason you are uncomfortable with me, you can ask for someone else. Some people don't like Jewish lawyers, but I don't stop till I get what you want!"

"No. No. You're okay by me," Eddie stammered. "I just wanna know what I'm in for. What did I do?"

"It has not been proven that you did anything. It is alleged that you may be the perpetrator of the rape homicide in Strobe Park."

"Rape? Homicide?" he shouted loudly, jumping up from the couch. "No, no, not me!" Eddie shouted again. "I haven't been near Strobe Park."

"Whoa. Calm down and remain seated, Mr. Wheeler. I said *alleged*. At this time, all they have is circumstantial evidence—fibers that appear to match your sweater and some hairs that also apparently match. You see," he explained with confidence, "alleged, the 'A' word. Don't worry."

"Don't worry? It's not your ass locked up in this place."

"Eddie, Eddie, listen to me, please. DNA is not your enemy. If you are innocent, you will walk out of here a free man. I'll have you out of here in thirty days, six weeks maximum. You'll be seeing a lot of me. In the meantime, enjoy your luxurious pad."

"What kinda jail is this anyway?" Eddie asked.

"It's a new program being tested by the Department of Corrections. The program studies the effects of a nonthreatening restrained environment and its impact on long-term rehabilitation. Just another federal grant."

"I'll try, thanks," replied Eddie as his counsel stood to leave.

After listening to his attorney and knowing that he was innocent, Eddie felt encouraged— until he heard that damn dead bolt again; it was a constant reminder of his captivity.

Chapter 7

Sarah was sorting through stacks of donated clothing when Rhonda came through the back door.

"Hi," she said. "What are you doing?"

"Oh, hi, Rhonda. I'm separating these by size and gender. It's been so cold lately these clothes are a godsend. You know, Rhonda, you have also been a godsend. We feel so blessed to have you with us."

"I enjoy the opportunity to help make a difference," she said, a little embarrassed by the compliment. "I am lucky to have met Pablo, who really is responsible for my volunteering."

"Not lucky, my dear; the Lord works in mysterious ways his wonders to perform."

One of her endless Bible quotes, Rhonda thought to herself and then tried to steer their conversation in a different direction. "Sarah," she asked, "have you heard anything about some of the street people disappearing?"

"Oh my." She laughed. "They are all missing from somewhere. The very nature of the transient is to keep moving. Here today, someplace else tomorrow. The sheep shall stray from the flock but, like the prodigal son, will someday return, and we will welcome them home with loving hearts.

"Remember, my dear: the lambs may stray, but the Good Shepherd will bring them home again. It's like the words in 'Amazing Grace': 'I once was lost, but now I'm found. I was blind, but now I see.'" She closed her eyes and smiled. "So, you see, my dear, don't worry about the ones who stray. They will be fine. Faith." She smiled. "You must put your faith in the Lord."

Not wishing to continue the old-time Gospel hour, Rhonda asked, "So what can I do today?"

"Well," replied Sarah, raising her eyebrows, "how do you deal with the sight of blood?"

"Fine, if it isn't mine," Rhonda answered with a smile.

"Good. We take a sample from everybody who comes through the door."

"For what purpose?" asked Rhonda.

"HIV," Sarah said in a tone that bordered on irritation. "We offer AIDS testing. You see," she explained, "some people get it in an innocent way, like blood transfusions. Some get it by using infected needles. But," she mumbled in a hushed, angry tone, her eyes narrowing, "most people get it the evil way—the men with men way. AIDS is God's punishment to those fornicating devils."

Rhonda thought for a moment that Sarah might pass out, the way she was beginning to hyperventilate.

Rhonda interrupted, again endeavoring to change the subject, "When can I get started?"

"Soon. A volunteer nurse is on the way over right now. In the meantime, you can go talk to the people in the dining room and recreation area. It's important that you convince them to participate. You may need to prod them a little.

"Of course," she added, "most of them, for obvious reasons, have no fear of needles. Each person will be given ten dollars for participating. That should make it easier."

The first people Rhonda encountered were Billy and Willy playing checkers at a table near the windows.

"Hi. We going in the van again?" questioned Billy.

"No. But we will need you and Willy to give a

little blood today."

"Why? Somebody need some blood?"

"No, Billy. We just want a little bit of yours to make sure you're healthy," she explained patiently.

"Me and Billy, we healthy. We don't do drugs no more, Miss Rhonda. We are God's children. We are borned again. Besides, Miss Sarah already has our blood long time ago," Willy said as she went back to their game.

Next, Rhonda approached a middle-aged black man reading a three-month-old *Reader's Digest*. He was about six feet four inches tall and weighed maybe two hundred ten pounds. "I don't believe we've met," said Rhonda. "What's your name?"

He looked up from the magazine with an annoyed expression. "I know damned well we ain't never met, and my name is my business."

"Of course," she said, taking a deep breath and trying again. "We're collecting blood samples and testing for—"

"No!" he bellowed. "You ain't getting no muthafuckin' blood from me. If it means I can't come here no more, that's okay too. Them two Bible-thumpers been trying to get my soul since I been comin' here. Now they want my muthafuckin' blood. Ain't no white man ever give a damn 'bout my black ass. So why you give a damn now?"

"Sir, you are not obligated to be tested. I'm sorry I bothered you."

As she walked away, she heard him mumbling to himself. "Ain't nobody gives a fuck 'bout Levi an' Jimmy neither. They just snatched their black asses off the street an' took 'em away. I won't never see 'em again."

Rhonda froze in her tracks. "What did you just say?" she demanded.

"Say what?" sneered the black man. "Now what you want, besides my blood?"

"You said something about somebody being snatched off the streets."

"Yeah, Levi and Jimmy. Blue took 'em."

"Who?"

"Blue—you know, po-leese!"

"How do you know it was the police?"

"I know a muthafuckin' po-leese van when I see one, an' I know what a muthafuckin' po-leese man looks like."

"Tell me about it, please," Rhonda said.

"Ain't much ta tell. We was down at the gallery ridin' the horse. Ya dig?"

"The horse?" Rhonda asked confused.

"Shootin' heroin. You know what I'm sayin'? Jimmy took a little too much an' started pukin'. I seen the van round the corner, and I dropped back behind a dumpsta. They just drove up an' snatched their asses! Last I seen, Levi was shakin' like a dog shittin' peach pits, and Jimmy was bad sick."

"Then what happened?"

"I waited till the next morning and went over to the Seventy-First Precinct. They told me there ain't been no junkies brought in last night. I don't know why, but them cops be lyin' mutha-fuckers."

"Maybe not," said Rhonda.

"Say what?"

"I know the captain at the precinct. I'll look into it."

"Uh-oh. Here comes mutha superior. I gotta split 'fore she whips a little jeezes on me."

Sarah frowned slightly as she joined Rhonda. "The nurse is here. We can use your help now. What did Moses want?"

"Moses?"

"Yes, what a wonderful Christian name wasted on a godless heathen," Sarah uttered with contempt.

Rhonda did not answer.

As Rhonda left to join the nurse, she remembered a Sunday school story about Moses leading his people to the Promised Land. Maybe this Moses could help lead her to some answers.

***

The man picked up his cell phone after one ring and waited.

"It's me, the Magician," said the voice on the other end. "This may be something. It may be nothing. But a new volunteer at the mission, a young broad, is asking questions about missing people. I followed her to the *City Voice*."

"That's not a good sign. Okay, good work," said the man. "Leave her a message, one she'll understand. Then try to find out what she knows and who she's been talking to. It's probably nothing ... But if there's a problem ... solve it ... You know what I'm saying?"

"I will," said the Magician with an evil grin. "I make problems disappear—it's what I do."

***

The Magician, with little effort, unlocked the door to apartment 303 and entered. He noted the apartment was furnished with a small couch, a love seat, and an overstuffed chair, which appeared to be of thrift-store quality. A side table contained a picture of two elderly people and a young twenty-something woman— *a family picture*, he mused. No table in the kitchen but two bar stools at the counter. Off the kitchen was a screened-in balcony containing a couple of wicker chairs and matching coffee table. The bedroom was sparse, with a small desk and a double bed. Over the desk hung a framed diploma from Davidson College, with the name Rhonda Wells.

The intruder opened the middle desk drawer, finding a signed contract from the *City Voice*, along with an opened letter from her mother. He stuffed the letter in his pocket—addresses of loved ones could be helpful in his line of work.

He saw a sudden movement to his left and turned to see a harmless calico cat on the bed. He coaxed the friendly feline with, "Here kitty, kitty." He picked up the cat and began to scratch behind her ears. "Nice kitty," he said, walking out on the balcony. Without a second thought, he whipped out his ever-present switchblade knife and then thought to himself, *So much for the proverbial nine lives.*

Before leaving her apartment, the Magician stopped to write a message on the refrigerator door. He mused over his poetic irony of using a magic marker to deliver his message.

When he finished, he helped himself to a beer, along with a piece of leftover meatloaf. Then making sure the door was locked before returning to his car, he waited and watched for her surprise homecoming.

***

Jack Rollins entered the building by the back door and took his seat again behind the screen. He thought, *It's finally beginning to take shape.* The Beau Monde Society now had ten new core members prepared to fulfill their secret pledge to save the world from mediocrity.

"It's time, Charles. You can let the doctors enter and take their seats."

When all the applicants were seated, the host appeared again behind the screen.

"Gentlemen," said the silhouette behind the screen, "it has taken three long years to assemble this team. The process is nearly complete. You have all now been accepted and informed of every facet of the operation. Nothing has been withheld except the identity of certain people, one being myself. This is by careful design. It is critical that you follow every procedure to the letter, adhering to all the rules, especially when off duty. Never discuss your work with an outsider. You will be watched; you will be tested. One of your cocandidates took my admonishment lightly, and he is no longer with us—thus, the reason for unidentified colleagues watching all activity.

"The long-awaited project begins tonight. You and your colleagues will receive a daily work schedule. Teams will be set up based upon orders received and the area of your expertise."

"There will be extensive cross-training. You are the best in your respective fields, so you will be asked to teach each other from time to time. You will receive a monthly statement with the amount of accrual in your retirement account beyond your base compensation. It will be substantial.

"That is all I have for now. If you don't draw a case tonight, you are free for the evening. But remember your communication device. Never, I say never, ever, be without it. You are excused."

After everyone had left, the man behind the screen took the private elevator down to a limo where his loyal friend and chauffeur, Charles, was waiting.

Chapter 8

Rhonda sat at the table in front of the library waiting for Pablo. She was making notes for the next day's column, "Part II of the Plight of the Homeless," when she heard the familiar "Yo, Rhonda. I brought lunch." Pablo presented her with a paper sack from Shelly's Deli.

"Why, thank you, Pablo," she said as she proceeded to lay out their lunch. "Today I'm going to write about a very unique homeless person—one with ambition and a plan to rise above his situation. A man who does not make or accept excuses. A man who believes in a day's work for a day's pay."

"Yeah, who's that?" Pablo asked as he raised his napkin to his lips.

"You," she replied. "Of course, I'll use a fictitious name to protect your identity."

"A what to protect my what?" he joked.

"A different name, you know, so you won't be

bothered by the publicity."

"Bothered? I can use the publicity. It pays to advertise. Anybody wants to invest, tell 'em to leave a message at J-3."

Rhonda shook her head and smiled. "I should know you'd think like an entrepreneur."

"Hey, watch what you're calling me, lady," he shot back with mock anger.

"Seriously," Rhonda began. "I need to get into your head, so to speak. Find out what drives you. Learn about your background. You previously told me you came from Costa Rica. What brought you to the United States?"

"Okay by me," Pablo interrupted, "but only if I can get into your head—you know, ask you a few questions. Like they say, what's good for the goose is good for the duck."

"The gander," she said laughing. "What's good for the goose is good for the gander."

"Whatever, but you know what I'm sayin'."

"Okay, that's fair. What do you want to ask me?"

"Well, where did you come from?"

"Brookline, Massachusetts, near Boston."

"Any brothers or sisters?"

"No. I'm an only child."

"Oh, so you were spoiled ...   How 'bout a

boyfriend. You got a boyfriend?"

"Well, sort of."

"Whaddaya mean, sort of?" he asked, unable to hide his disappointment.

"He's a tennis pro. He accepted a teaching job in Florida, but New York is where it's happening in journalism. So, for now, it looks like a long-distance relationship. He left his cat with me for protection," she said with a smile. "His name is Topspin."

"Your boyfriend's name is Topspin?"

Laughing, Rhonda replied, "No, silly. The cat. My boyfriend's name is Todd, Todd Scott."

"Well, all I can say is Todd Scott better not leave you alone too long, or he's gonna lose a good woman, along with his cat," Pablo joked as he fidgeted with his napkin.

"Thank you, Pablo. That is a nice compliment. Now let's get started on your story."

"So, whaddaya wanna know?"

"You said you came from Costa Rica. Why?"

"First, it ain't easy leavin' Costa Rica. You don't just get in a plane and fly to the United States. I was lucky. My old man was an American citizen, and he signed the papers for me to come and sent me a ticket. I guess he was feeling guilty 'bout leavin' me and my mother.

He was in the military when they met. When his time was up, he went home. He promised to bring us later. But he waited nineteen years. By then, my mother and stepfather had a buncha kids. Anyways, I felt like odd man out. So, I came here to live with my old man."

"How did that work out?" Rhonda asked.

"Not wortha shit. He drank a lot. When he came home drunk, he'd start layin' a buncha shit on me like I didn't appreciate all he done for me, bringing me to the greatest country in the world. Like I should kiss his ass every day. So, one day I told him I didn't appreciate him 'cause he was a deadbeat asshole who never gave a shit about me or my mother. And because of him, I was always the family bastard. So, when he started whackin' me upside the head and told me to get the fuck out . . . I left and never went back. Gone! With nothin' but the clothes on my back. Ain't seen him since. Could be dead for all I know."

"So, how did you survive on your own?" Rhonda asked.

"It wasn't easy. I couldn't talk good English. I did whatever I could—ya know, odd jobs. Made enough to get by. One day I was sweeping up the garage at Ace Custom Vans when Hal, the owner, says I can stay in this gutted-out van behind the shop in the backyard. Says I'd be cheaper than a guard dog. He let me run an electrical cord from his building. I got a hot plate, a little heater, and one light bulb, except not all at once unless I want to blow a breaker. The mechanics get in an hour before they open, so I take a shower and shave in the locker room. I wash my clothes at the laundry place once a week. Ain't no excuse for being dirty, even if you're poor.

"It don't cost me much to live, so everything I earn I put in the bank for my car company. I'm getting pretty close too. You know, my old man was right about one thing."

"What was that?" Rhonda asked.

"That this is the best damn country in the world! If I ever see him, I'll probably tell him that."

"You may not have to."

"Yeah, why?"

"As long as I'm going to use your real name, he might read about you in the paper."

"Could happen. But my old man don't read much. Okay what else ya wanna know?" asked Pablo as he started to pace back and forth near the picnic table.

"That's enough for my column. But I want to know if you've ever met a man at J-3 named Moses."

"Moses, that big black dude? Yeah, I know Moses. Had a future with the Jets, a defensive back, till he started hittin' the heroin harder than his opponents. He hung out with a couple of junkies, Levi and Jimmy."

"Exactly," Rhonda went on. "Moses claims they were taken away in an NYPD van. However, I called Captain Kruger personally, and he said there is no record of two homeless people being arrested in their precinct."

"What about another precinct?"

"No way. The captain said they never make arrests outside their jurisdiction."

"You putting a lotta faith in a cop if ya ask me."

"He's tough, Pablo, but I'm beginning to have a positive feeling about him. So far, he has done what he promised. He returns all my calls. I believe he cares—even if he is, in my opinion, as conservative as my dad."

"So, what's next?" asked Pablo.

"The captain wants to meet with you, me, Moses, and anybody else who may have some information. However, he wants to wait for reports from his undercover detectives and the confidential informants, probably early next week."

"Okay by me. Just leave a message with Sarah at J-3."

"I'd better get back if I'm going to make deadline. Remember when you're famous, I helped!"

***

As Rhonda returned to the office, she kept thinking about all Pablo had told her and how amazed she was that he'd overcome so much at such a young age. She knew she wanted to be sure the column reflected his character.

She closed up her desk after spending time researching material for her next column, left the building, and headed home.

Rhonda felt somewhat euphoric on the drive home, satisfied with the progress she'd made today. She was planning on a simple dinner, a relaxing bath, and a call to Todd. She stopped at the grocery store to pick up a few canned goods, some microwave dinners, and fresh fruit, along with a bottle of wine.

Rhonda had to park one block away from her apartment, but her mood was not dampened by the inconvenience. She struggled with her briefcase, her laptop computer, and a sack of groceries, all of which she was determined to carry in one trip.

She entered her apartment backward, leaning against the door due to her cumbersome load. She set the grocery bag on the counter and withdrew a bottle of chardonnay. As she turned toward the refrigerator, she froze, dropping the bottle of wine, which shattered in all directions on the tile floor.

She stared in horror at the message on the refrigerator written with a black felt-tip marker:

You questioned this.

You questioned that.

Now your curiosity killed your cat.

Rhonda felt like she would faint and needed some air. She ran to the sliding glass doors leading out to her small balcony. As she opened the vertical blinds and fumbled with the latch, she saw the headless carcass of Topspin.

She screamed and felt the vomit force itself upward in her throat. She ran into the bathroom, falling to her knees in front of the commode.

It was then that she came face-to-face with the cat's head staring up at her. She swirled to her left just in time to throw up into the bathtub. She could barely see through her tears, gasping for breath.

"I've got to get away," she said out loud. "I might be next.

"Oh my God. Oh my God," she kept repeating.

She ran from the apartment, leaving the door open, and was halfway to her car before remembering the car keys she'd left on the kitchen counter.

As she ran back in, she slipped on the wet floor, falling on the broken glass. With blood coming from both hands and knees, she grabbed the keys and fled down the stairs, sprinting to her car. Her hands were trembling so badly it took several attempts before she got the key into the ignition. Crying, praying, and cursing at the same time, she sped away.

Rhonda drove with difficulty, tears spilling down her face, trying to speed dial the Seventy-First Precinct. Now shaking uncontrollably, she pulled into a strip mall, attempting to gain control of her emotions as she parked in front of a busy CVS drugstore.

Before redialing, she sat motionless, concentrating on deep breathing to calm her nerves.

After several rings, the desk sergeant answered. "Seventy-First Precinct."

"Captain Kruger," cried Rhonda, trying desperately to control her emotions but failing miserably.

"The captain has left for the day."

"Then give me his home number," Rhonda blurted, her voice shaking. "Please. My life is in danger," she pleaded.

"Who are you? Where are you? I can send a patrol car there immediately."

"I need Captain Kruger. He knows me. I don't want a patrol car . . . I'm sorry. I didn't mean to yell. Please, I need to speak with Captain Kruger . . . please."

Suddenly, there was nothing on the line.

"Oh my God. Please don't hang up." Rhonda sobbed. "Please."

"I'm not going to hang up on you," the officer assured her. "Give me your name and number. I'll call Captain Kruger's home and ask him to call you."

"Oh, thank you. Thank you," Rhonda whispered.

"If he's not home, I'll call you back myself."

"Thank you so much," said Rhonda, giving her name and number.

Trying to stop shaking, she hung up and sat

there, without moving, desperately attempting to put the picture of Topspin out of her mind. After a few minutes, which seemed more like an hour, her phone rang. Forgetting to switch to hands-free mode, she dropped the phone.

By the third ring, Rhonda answered. "Hello," she whispered, although she had no idea she was whispering.

"Rhonda, what's wrong?" asked Captain Kruger.

"Oh, thank God it's you!" she cried. "My apartment has been broken into. They killed Topspin, my cat. They threw his head in my toilet. His body is on the patio, and there is blood everywhere. They left me a threatening note, and now I'm afraid they're going to kill me," she cried hysterically.

"Rhonda," he said. "Where are you now? Did you leave your apartment?"

"Yes, and I pulled into a strip mall and parked in front of a CVS drugstore."

"Did you notice if anyone followed you?"

"No. I can't even remember if I looked around. All I could think of was to get out of there."

"Listen to me very carefully. Nobody is going to kill you. You've left your apartment. That's good. You're safe for now, okay?"

"Yes, but I'm so scared."

"I know, but you must calm down."

"Okay, I'm calm," she babbled. "What should I do?"

"Go to the Seventy-First Precinct now, but do not take a direct route. Make several turns and watch for anybody following you. Call back if you need me."

She pulled out into traffic and noticed a Jeep Cherokee behind her, followed by a bread truck. The Jeep made a left turn, while the truck continued down the street. Rhonda saw another vehicle, a large black sedan, but it was too far back to identify. Seconds later, she looked again in the rearview mirror, and the black sedan was gaining on the truck. She turned right at the next light and the bread truck continued straight. Now the black sedan was getting closer, so close that she could see a tall bald man behind the wheel. Her foot began shaking so badly that she could barely keep it on the accelerator. She made a quick left and looked in the mirror; he was still there. One more left, and she was now on the road to the precinct. She hit the speed dial on her hands-free phone. Captain Kruger answered on the first ring.

"You were right. A black sedan is following me."

"How close are you to the precinct?"

Rhonda answered as she sped up, trying to put distance between her and the sedan, "I don't know, maybe two or three miles ... Oh no, thank God," she cried.

"What? What's happening?"

"I'm being pulled over by the police."

"Good. Stay on the line with me," he said.

As the young officer approached her car, Rhonda noted that the back sedan continued on. It was a Lexus. Rhonda lowered her window.

"Do you know why I stopped you?" the officer asked.

"No, but I'm glad you did," she answered, which prompted a quizzical look from the young officer.

"You exceeded the speed limit, ran a red light, and your driving was erratic."

"You're not going to believe this ... I've been talking with Captain Kruger of the Seventy-First Precinct on speaker mode," she explained. "He's on the line with me right now."

The officer rolled his eyes in a cynical manner.

"Seriously," she argued, seeing the officer's name above his shield. "Captain, this is Officer Wescott with me. Will you tell him what's going on?" She handed the phone to the young officer.

"Captain, this is Wescott. What's the deal?"

"I'll explain later, but please escort this young lady to the station and let her park in the employee's lower garage. I'll call ahead so they will be expecting you."

***

Rhonda sat filling out the police report in careful detail when Captain Kruger entered the room. At first glance, she didn't recognize him in his blue jeans and sweatshirt. She jumped up from her chair and hurried to meet him, wanting very much to hug him, as she felt relief just seeing him. Instead, she stopped short, directly facing him, and clasped both hands around her cheeks, tears welling up in her eyes.

"Thanks for being here for me, Captain. I'm so relieved to see you. I didn't know where else to turn."

"No problem. My wife is out with the grand-kids, and I felt I should be here. This appears to be more than a simple break-and-enter problem. You obviously stumbled onto something, and somebody thinks you know more than you should. The important thing now is to keep you out of sight until we can get a handle on things. Let's go into my office and figure out what to do next. Have a seat while I get us some coffee. Cream and sugar?"

"No thanks. Black will be fine."

While he was gone, Rhonda looked around his office, now familiar to her. She studied more carefully the pictures of his family. She began to realize that she liked him, seeing him more of an ally than an adversary.

"Here's what I would like to do," Garth began as he handed Rhonda a Styrofoam cup and settled into his chair. "It's highly unlikely, but someone could be watching for your car to exit the garage."

Sipping her coffee, Rhonda asked, "Could I get a ride in a cruiser to a hotel?"

"You could," Garth replied, running his fingers through his salt-and-pepper hair. "But I have a better idea. I have a friend, Gloria, who manages a safe house for battered women and women who have been rescued from human trafficking. You would be very safe there. Gloria is a sweetheart. You'll love her. Besides, hotels cost a fortune."

"Whatever you say, Captain. At this point, I'm a total basket case."

Garth took Rhonda to the shelter and introduced her to Gloria, making arrangements to pick her up in the morning.

Chapter 9

The Magician dialed the number on his cell phone. "Hey, boss, like you wanted, I've been tailing the broad who's been nosing around at the mission."

"And?" said the voice on the other end.

"Turns out she's a reporter—one of them bleeding heart types. She's writing a daily column on the homeless. Her real name is Rhonda Wells. Just wanted to let you know I left her a surprise message in her apartment this afternoon that she won't soon forget. Then I hung around to see her reaction. She must have freaked because she ran out of her apartment, jumped in her car, and took off."

"Did you follow her? Where did she go?"

"She must have called the police because a squad car pulled her over and then escorted her to the Seventy-First Precinct."

"Is that it?"

"Almost," he replied. "When I checked out her apartment, I found a business card on her kitchen counter for Captain Garth Kruger."

"I don't like this. These two people are becoming a problem. We will have to deal with them," his boss answered and then hung up.

***

Rhonda spent the night at the safe house but could not sleep. The thought of the maniac who'd been in her apartment brought visions of what he had done to her cat and what he intended to do to her, sending shivers down her spine. Sleep was out of the question. She lay there watching the clock turn hour after hour. She formulated a plan for tomorrow.

At exactly eight o'clock, Garth's silver Taurus drove up.

"Good morning, Rhonda. Have you had anything to eat?"

"Yes. Gloria is wonderful. She provided a delicious breakfast."

"So, have you thought about what you are going to do today?"

"Yes. When we get back to the precinct to get my car, the first thing I'm going to do is find a dealership, any dealership, and trade it in for something inconspicuous."

They walked to the car. Garth opened the passenger door and then walked around and got in. "Now, after you trade your car, then what?"

"I'm going to find a new apartment and go pick up my belongings."

"Wrong. You aren't going to go near your apartment. Just make a list of what you want."

"I don't want any of the furniture, just a few personal belongings, my clothes, and especially my laptop. I can't work without it."

Rhonda noticed the captain kept looking in his rearview mirror as they were driving to the precinct. "Is something wrong?"

"No. Why do you ask?"

"You keep looking in your rearview mirror."

"I'm just being observant. Or as my dad used to say, 'A good cop needs to have eyes in the back of his head,'" Garth explained as he glanced at her. "Okay. As soon as you're settled, I'll make sure your stuff is delivered to your new place. By the way, have you made arrangements with your employer?"

"Yes. I spoke with Jim this morning and explained everything. He was very concerned and insisted that I work from home. He also added that he would like to have a conversation with you when it's convenient."

They pulled into the lower deck of the parking garage next to Rhonda's car. As they got out of the car, Garth turned to her and said, "We both have our work cut out for us today. Don't hesitate to call me for any reason at all."

"I will. And thank you for everything," said Rhonda as she slid behind the wheel of her little VW beetle. As she waved goodbye, she said, "I'll call you with my new address."

Rhonda drove away and headed for the Honda dealership on Liberty Avenue. The light turned red, and while she was waiting, she looked into her rearview mirror, and her heart sank. A black Lexus was approaching in the left lane.

As the car passed her, she breathed a sigh of relief when she noticed the driver was a middle-aged woman. "My God, I'm jumping at shadows," she scolded herself.

One block ahead, she pulled into the dealership, parked her VW, and walked around the yard looking at used cars. What caught her eye was a white Honda hatchback with very dark tinted windows. She wasn't interested in any extra accessories. She didn't bother to haggle over the price or the amount of trade-in offered on her car. She wrote a check for the entire amount. She was the type of customer all car salesmen pray for.

After her check cleared through the bank, she drove off feeling very secure in her new ride.

Fortunately, she found a furnished apartment that she liked. She wrote a check to the manager for first and last months' rent, along with a security deposit. She sat in her new living room and texted her new address to Captain Kruger.

That afternoon, an officer delivered several boxes filled with items from the list she had given Garth. She spent the rest of the evening getting things put away and stocked her kitchen from a market within walking distance from her apartment. She made a short list of remaining items she would need.

Topping the list was a flat-screen television, which she planned to pick up the following day. For a brief moment, she actually contemplated changing her long blonde hair to a short brunette cut. Then on second thought, she said aloud, "No. I'm not going to let those bastards control my life."

***

Garth was pleased that Rhonda's new address was in a low crime area; it was an excellent location for a single woman. He spent the rest of the day catching up on a major backlog of tasks that he'd failed to get to because of Rhonda's crisis with the stalker. He had a meeting with his lieutenant and his drug task force. He read over the reports of his two undercover narcs. He needed to appease Wade Newman's laundry list of things to bitch about. Before the day was over, he found himself walking around his office mulling over the connection between some missing homeless people and a reporter's article in the *City Voice* and how it could be connected to Rhonda's home invasion. One thing he knew. Rhonda has opened Pandora's box.

Garth cleared his desk and left for the day. He and Susan had a quiet evening, watched a movie on Netflix, shared a glass of wine, and turned in for the night.

***

The next morning, Garth was up before Susan made coffee and sat reading the *City Voice*.

He looked up when Susan walked into the kitchen.

"Good morning, big guy. I see you're up early."

"I slept better last night than I have in a long time. Must have been the company and that movie with the happy ending."

Susan smiled and then asked, "Any good news in that paper you're reading?"

"Yes. The Rangers have won four games straight."

"You're a trip." She laughed as she poured herself coffee. "We could be under a nuclear attack, and you'd be worried that it might melt the ice at Madison Square Garden."

"That could never happen. The whole Russian Army is playing there now! But I do have good news for you," said Garth.

"And that is?"

"I'm taking your Toyota to work today. Pete in the motor pool will mount and balance your new tires," said Garth as he sipped coffee and scanned the paper. "He'll do it during his break. We don't want to be accused of spending tax dollars on car repairs for the captain's wife, now do we?"

"Umm . . . That's nice of Pete to give up his off time," Susan commented.

"I know," Garth responded. "I'll offer to pay

him, and he'll put on his I'm-insulted, what-are-
friends-for act. Then I'll put a bottle of Old Crow
in his car under the passenger seat. That's the
way it works," he said, shaking his head and
smiling.

"Well, anyway, Mr. Hockey Guy, I'm glad
you're leaving me the Taurus. I'm taking Chipper and Katie to the mall. Can you switch the
kids' car seats to the Taurus for me?"

Garth answered, "Sure thing."

"It seems Grandpa promised Chipper a
Ranger jersey, which he reminds me of daily."

"Oh, damn. I keep forgetting. Thanks, honey.
Make sure it's a Brad Richards, number nineteen. And get one for Katie too."

"Great. And what position do you have in
mind for her?"

"I don't know. Maybe goalie."

"Well, she wants ballet slippers."

"Like father, like daughter." Garth smirked
with a snicker.

"Okay, enough. Don't start on Ben."

"I'm sorry, honey. I like Ben. I like him a lot.
It's just that he's so easy to pick on."

"All well and good. Pick on somebody your
own size," she said as she slid her arms around
his neck and kissed him lightly and then in-

creasing with more passion.

"Umm . . . maybe I should call in sick today," he said softly.

"Go. Get out of here. I'm going to the mall with the kids."

"Okay, okay. I'm leaving. See ya. Love ya. Bye."

"Hey, big guy," Susan said.

"Yeah?"

"Let's be careful out there."

After Garth left, Susan finished folding a load of towels and began loading the dishwasher with the breakfast dishes. She smiled to herself as she thought how Garth would tease her if he saw how she scrubbed each piece clean with soapy water and then rinsed it before placing it in the dishwasher. *We have such a great marriage*, she thought to herself. *Of course, we disagree on several occasions, but we respect each other. It's so simple. Accept what is, let go of what was, and have faith in what will be.*

Before leaving, she made the bed and then called her daughter.

"Lisa, I'll be leaving in a few minutes to pick up Chipper and Katie for our trip to the mall. I may be a few minutes late returning them so I can run the Taurus through the car wash along the way back. Your dad will appreciate this, since he's always too busy to do it himself. Besides, the kids love watching the brushes and foam."

"No problem, Mom. I'll have them ready for you when you get here."

"Great, see you in a few."

Susan stepped out into a warm spring day, enjoying the feel of the warm sun on her face.

Being safety conscious, she went through her own little checklist. Car seat for Katie, check. Large car seat for Chipper—he called it the big boy seat—check. Adjust mirrors, seat, and seat belt. "Okay. All systems go," she said to herself with a smile. She backed out the driveway, turned on the radio to her favorite music station, and headed down the road.

***

Garth was sitting at his desk when the phone rang; it was his daughter Lisa.

"Dad, have you heard from Mom?"

"No. Why?"

"I'm worried. She should have been here an hour ago and never arrived. And I can't get her on her cell."

"Don't worry, honey. She probably stopped

somewhere and left her phone in the car. Keep in touch, but I have to go now. There's somebody here to see me."

Garth waved the man in.

"Captain Kruger. My name is Matthew Allen, NYPD chaplain."

"Yes, Chaplain. What can I do for you?"

"I'm afraid I have bad news for you, and there is no easy way to say this."

Garth's demeanor changed. "What it is?"

"There was a single car accident with a silver Taurus registered in your name. The driver, identified as Susan Kruger, passed away on the way to the hospital."

Garth put his head on his desk, pounding with both fists and saying, "It's all my fault. She should have been driving her car."

The chaplain walked around the desk, put his hand on Garth's shoulder, and remained silent.

"I can't believe this. I can't believe this. I need to call my daughter right now."

Garth could hardly speak as Lisa answered the phone. "Lisa, Mom had an accident, and she didn't make it," he said, sobbing uncontrollably.

"Dad," Lisa answered with a hoarse voice. "I

need you. Please come now."

"I will, sweetheart. I'll be there as soon as possible. I have to go to the hospital first." Garth hung up the phone, laid his head on the desk, and sobbed.

The chaplain patted Garth's back and said, "I'm so sorry for your loss. Is there anything I can do?"

"No, Chaplain. Thanks so much for coming."

The chaplain said, "Here's my card." He patted Garth on his back one last time. "Call me if there is anything I can do."

The chaplain quietly left the office.

***

The church was packed with friends and family for the memorial service of Susan Kruger. On a small table to the right of the altar sat a beautiful, ornate urn beside a large framed color photo of Susan showing her radiant smile. Garth sat in the front row with his daughter, Lisa; her husband, Ben; and their two children, Chipper and Katie. Garth broke down in tears often, thinking that the two little ones beside him would never see their grandma again, and nor would she see them. They couldn't understand what had happened—only that Grandma was in heaven.

Garth sat silently while he listened to countless testimonies from people who had known Susan well—her childhood friends, teachers and professors, sorority sisters, and neighbors. Many who were present, Garth had never met. One after another, they stood up to sing the praises of their dear friend Susan. During each testimony, Garth found it difficult to listen and broke down sobbing. It was wonderful to hear. But at the same time, it was brutal knowing that he would never see his Susan again. Without exception, everyone praised her big heart, positive attitude, and gentle spirit.

The people filed out of the church, approaching Garth. He stood at the back, shook every hand, and accepted every warm embrace. He listened to the countless expressions of love and sympathy: "She was an awesome person, a wonderful mother, the perfect grandmother. Our prayers are with you and your family." On and on it went.

Yet, Garth was in no hurry for it to end. As long as he continued to hear and talk about Susan, he didn't have to face the incredible loneliness that lay ahead.

"I'm so sorry," said the young woman with the

long blonde hair and sunglasses. He recognized Rhonda's voice.

"Rhonda, thank you for coming."

"I can't image how you feel," she said, tears streaming down her cheeks.

Garth hugged her close. "Please follow us back to my house. I want you to meet my family, and we need to talk." His eyes were red and a little swollen from crying, and he was on the verge of tears again.

Rhonda realized she was seeing a different Captain Kruger, one who was vulnerable and genuine, like a family member.

***

As the last car drove out of the church parking lot, no one noticed the black Lexus following in the distance.

***

Rhonda left the church and followed the friends and family to Garth's home for the reception.

Although she didn't know anybody but the captain and had never met Susan, Rhonda felt great sadness. She felt the Kruger family's deep grief as if it were her own. Rhonda's mind flashed back to the death of her father months earlier, and she found it difficult to hold back the tears. She walked over to the table set up in the living room and helped herself to a cup of coffee and a finger sandwich.

She watched the captain talking to a group of friends. When she caught his eye, he motioned her over and introduced her to his friends and then his family.

"Rhonda, this is my daughter, Lisa, and my son-in-law, Ben. Ben and Lisa, this is Rhonda. She's a journalist at the *City Voice*. We have been working on a case together."

Two beautiful children came running into the room. The boy sidled up to Garth and hugged his leg with one arm.

"This is Chipper," Garth said with a look of such unconditional love that it gave Rhonda goose bumps. "And this little princess is Katie." His warm smile said it all.

Katie hid behind her mother but peeked around to look at Rhonda. As she continued burying her face into her mother's dress, she whispered, "Did you know my grandma?"

It took a moment for Rhonda to compose herself. Kneeling down, she reached out as Katie, almost on cue, walked into her arms.

"I'm Chipper," said the little boy. "My grammie went to heaven. Do you know where heaven is?"

Garth immediately excused himself and went into the bedroom down the hall.

Ben left the women standing together. "I'm going to go see if there's anything I can do."

"You know, Rhonda, I have a feeling Dad and Ben are going to learn to like each other. Like Mom always said, 'Behind every dark cloud . . .'"

Some minutes later, Rhonda said to Lisa, "I should be going now. Would you please tell your dad when he feels up to it to give me a call?"

"Okay I will. It was nice meeting you, Rhonda. But I wish it was under different circumstances. Dad is on bereavement leave for the next couple of days, and Ben and I and the kids plan to spend as much time with him as possible."

Rhonda answered, "I understand. Take care. It was so nice to meet you and your family."

Rhonda left the reception, got in her car, and drove home. She was deep in thought agonizing over the pain and anguish she had just left behind. All she wanted to do at this point was go home and call her mom. She pulled into her parking spot and walked to her door.

The dark sedan drove past without slowing down.

Chapter 10

Rhonda was at her word processor working on her column when she was interrupted by her phone. It was Captain Kruger.

"How are you holding up?" she asked with genuine concern.

"I'm doing okay. Ben, Lisa, and the kids are smothering me with attention. Can't say I mind. How about you? How are you coping?"

"Well, I'm comfortable here. The paper has been very supportive. I'm writing from memory since I can't go near J-3 or the office."

"Rhonda, this may be something; it may be nothing. But I spoke to the officers who responded to the scene of Susan's accident. They believe the accident is somewhat suspicious. It was a clear dry day on a straight stretch of highway; no sign of skid marks. It looked to them like someone had forced the car off the road. We may never know. But it was my car Susan drove that day, and I may have been the target. Also, we're investigating the murder of Phillip Brown from a different angle now; maybe this is all somehow connected with Pablo's missing friend, Eddie Wheeler. We're going to get to the bottom of this—if it's the last thing I do. I want to meet your friend Pablo. I think he may point me in the right direction. How can I contact him?"

"Leave a message at J-3. I'm sure he'll get back to you. Tell him you're a friend of mine. You may want to talk to a guy by the name of Moses—a big black man, hates cops. He might not talk with you, but it's worth a try."

"Good. I'll do that. You have my home number and my personal cell. If you need me, don't hesitate to call. Another thing—be careful. These people play hardball. Keep your head up and your eyes open. I'll call you when I have something."

After Rhonda hung up, she sat at her desk to complete her column for tomorrow's edition. She stopped typing after a few minutes and realized that it was impossible for her to focus. *Maybe I'm just going stir-crazy cooped up in this small apartment*, she thought.

She walked over to the refrigerator, looked inside, and realized it was pretty empty except for the sandwich she spied. She remembered making it prior to the funeral, but she hadn't eaten because she was too nervous. She grabbed her purse and the car keys and put on her light blue hoodie as she left the apartment and locked the door. She backed out of her designated spot and glanced around. Her heart sank when she thought she saw a tall bald man across the street. But when she looked again, he wasn't there. She laughed at herself and thought, *I'm seeing shadows.*

She waited for the traffic to clear as she turned right, heading to the Ming Dynasty Restaurant, which had been recommended to her by some of her colleagues at the paper. She ordered chicken fried rice and an egg roll to go and sat down to wait. When her order was ready, she paid with her credit card and headed back to her car. She started the car, and as she put the car in reverse, there was a loud grinding noise coming from the engine. She didn't have any idea what it could be, but it sounded pretty bad.

She opened the glove compartment, where she had stored the bill of sale. She called the salesman, Steve Hall, and explained the situation. He was all apologetic and agreed to pick up her car at the restaurant and send a loaner there for her to use until they could fix or replace her car. While she waited, the restaurant staff cleared a small table for her, and she ate her lunch there.

She was pleased with the loaner, a black Honda Accord with tinted windows. She intended to return to her apartment but instead found herself driving in the direction of the J-3 Mission, certain that no one would recognize her in this loaner. Just to be sure, she put the hood of her jacket around her head, being careful to tuck in all her blonde hair.

Knowing this wasn't a wise move, Rhonda continued to cruise toward J-3 anyway. She was curious to see if Pablo or Willy and Billy were hanging out. As she approached the mission, she was surprised to see Sarah standing in the doorway talking to a tall dark man with a shaved head wearing sunglasses.

Oh my God, she thought. *That could be him!*

Get a grip, she chided herself. *Your mind is playing tricks*.

She drove past the mission and turned left and then made another left. "It couldn't be. Don't panic. Be calm. Nobody knows this car.

The windows are tinted. Turn left, go back, and check it out."

Rhonda drove toward J-3 again. The man was gone; it was probably nothing. She was beginning to feel a little silly, as well as embarrassed. "God, Rhonda," she scolded out loud, "your mind is playing tricks on you."

She decided to go back to her apartment and work on her column. Glancing in her rearview mirror before turning, she gasped. "No, this cannot be." She put her turn signal on and waited for an oncoming truck to pass. A black Lexus was on her bumper. Rhonda turned left, preparing to outrun the car, when she realized the Lexus had continued straight ahead. She spotted a Starbucks on the right and pulled in.

She ordered a mocha latte and sat in a far corner at a small table, mulling over what she had seen and what she could do next. If that was the same man who'd followed her, why would he be at the mission speaking with Sarah? What could be the connection? Rhonda sipped her drink and began to hatch a plan to get to the truth, whatever it was.

She drove back to her apartment, intending to put her plan to the test.

***

Rhonda picked up the phone and dialed the J-3 Mission.

Sarah answered. "Praise the Lord," she declared. "Where in the world have you been? We've been so worried about you."

"I had to go upstate for a while. Something came up unexpectedly, and I didn't have time to call you before I left," Rhonda said.

"Well, we sure did miss you around here. When will you back?"

"Tomorrow morning for sure. I have an eye appointment with Clearview Optical at three o'clock this afternoon at the Park Side Mall, and I'll never get back in time today."

"Oh, not to worry," Sarah assured her. "We can get by until tomorrow. Don't you worry about a thing, honey. Remember God loves you. And so do we."

Rhonda hung up the phone and thought to herself, *The trap is set. Will the mouse take the cheese?*

***

Rhonda sat in the food court on the second level of the mall, affording her an excellent view of Clearview Optical below. From her vantage point, she sat with a cup of coffee and a copy of the *National Enquirer*, which helped conceal her identity. After all, what self-respecting journalist would read that? She also wore a brunette wig with a large floppy hat shading the top half of her face. Even if he recognized her, she could be out the exit and gone before he could get to the escalator, which was halfway down the length of the mall.

She was feeling pretty secure—until the tall man walked up to a frozen yogurt shop not fifteen feet away. She rested her chin in the palm of her left hand and let her hair fall over her face while pretending to read the magazine.

Rhonda raised her eyes, and the man now was standing less than ten feet away. *Oh my God. What if he asks me a question or wants to talk?* She was unable to move if she had to. Realizing she hadn't taken a breath, all she could do was stare at his shoes as they began to move ever closer.

She closed her eyes and waited. Maybe he would do it quickly without pain. *Oh, why didn't I listen to Garth and just stay home?*

Her heart was pounding as her fear accelerated. She heard the sound of his shoes on the terrazzo floor as he inched closer and then pivoted slightly as he walked on past. She found the nerve to peek and saw him walking stealthily toward the down escalator. *Don't move. Don't breathe*, she told herself. *Wait until he reaches the lower level.*

The man stopped at the bottom of the escalator, bought a *USA Today* from a vending machine, and sat down on a bench near the entrance of Clearview Optical.

Rhonda tried to walk away as casually as possible and did for about three paces. Then she bolted like a scared rabbit once she was out of sight. As Rhonda drove away from the mall, she had no doubt whatsoever that Saint John and sweet Sarah Barnes were not on the side of God or the law. *But why? What in the name of all that's holy are they up to?* she wondered. *Or more likely, what are they up to in the name of God?*

With that unsavory character still back at the mall, she felt somewhat safe for now. *So why not stake out J-3?* she thought.

It was a quarter after five in the evening when Rhonda parked across the street about one half block away. She had no plan except to follow the Barneses and play it by ear. Forty-five minutes later, their beat-up, rusty yellow Dodge pulled out of the driveway and headed east, belching smoke.

That old rust bucked looks like it won't make it around the block, let alone back and forth to work every day, Rhonda thought as she pulled out into traffic, keeping at least one car between them and being careful not to get too close.

About three-quarters of a mile, the beat-up car turned right as the light changed to red, and the car in front of her stopped. "Shit," she grumbled impatiently. After what seemed like an eternity, the light changed, and Rhonda turned. There was no yellow car in sight. "Damn." She had lost them.

Well, she decided, *I can always do this another day.*

Suddenly, to her left, she saw a bright color. It was the rear end of a yellow Dodge chugging up the incline of a parking garage. She turned around and went back. *Why in the hell would they be parking here?* There were no residential buildings nearby, only shops and light manufacturing, which were all closed for the night.

She pulled the parking ticket from the electronic dispenser and followed the cloud of smoke.

On level three, she saw the car pull into a space and stop. She pulled into a distant space to watch. What happened next was beyond bizarre. John and Sarah got out of the old rust bucket and got into a fancy Mercedes 500SEL. "This is crazy," she whispered to herself. Her father drove a car like that, and she remembered a price tag of something like $100,000. Now those unholy rollers were indeed rolling in style as they headed down towards the exit ramp.

Rhonda waited until they were one level below before moving out in cautious pursuit. She waited until the Mercedes turned right out of the garage and then hurriedly paid her parking fee, determined not to lose sight of them again.

The Mercedes headed west toward the Hudson River on State Route 25 for three miles or so, continuing on through the towns of Palisades Park and Englewood, both in New Jersey. *God, I hope they're not going upstate*, she worried to herself as she noticed her gas gauge hovering near empty. They entered Interstate 87 North when suddenly she heard a bong and noticed that the low fuel indicator light blinked on. She figured, at thirty miles per gallon, surely there must be at least a gallon of gas left in the tank.

Up ahead, the turn signal indicated that John and Sarah would exit at White Plains. *Who could they possibly know in this affluent community?* she wondered. *Maybe they were returning the Mercedes to whoever loaned it as a favor,* she told herself. *There could be any number of explanations.* The car turned right on Marshall Street and then right again on Sterling. About halfway down the block, the Mercedes turned into a driveway on the left. To Rhonda's surprise, the garage door opened automatically, and they pulled in.

"Holy shit. They live here?" she said under her breath as she watched the garage door come down. Rhonda went on down the street, being careful not to appear suspicious of them or the neighbors. She turned around at the end of the street and drove past the house one more time. It was a two-story brick estate on a large lot, beautifully landscaped and professionally manicured. *What they earn at the mission could not even pay for the yard service in this neighborhood,* she thought. There was nothing more she could do.

I might as well get back home and share the news with Garth, she decided. *But I'd better find a gas station first.*

Her mind raced as she left the street; she almost had a head-on collision with an oncoming car. Rhonda swerved just in time to avoid a black Lexus. *If that's our man,* she thought, *he must be on his way to a meeting with John and Sarah Barnes.*

Rhonda filled her car with gas at the first convenience store she found. She vowed never to let the gauge fall below half a tank again. She shuddered to think what might have happened had she been stranded, out of gas, and walking down the dark road as the Lexus drove past.

She'd had enough drama for one day and didn't want to deal with it alone any longer, so she punched in the captain's number.

He answered on the second ring.

"Captain, it's me."

"Hi, Rhonda. What's up?" he asked in a tone that said *I'm glad to be talking to somebody.*

"I don't know where to begin," she said. "But I need to talk with you. Is it okay if I come by tonight?"

"No. It would be better if we met someplace else. If my house is being watched, they could get a make on your new car. It's very, very important that you stay out of sight for a while. Where are you now?"

"Up near White Plains."

"Okay," he said. "Go home to your apartment.

I'll make sure I'm not being followed and meet you there in about an hour."

Rhonda had been home fifteen minutes when Garth knocked on the door.

"Hi. Thanks for coming," she said as she gave him a quick hug.

"No problem. I'm going bonkers in that empty house. I keep expecting to see Susan coming into the den with coffee or a fat-free yogurt in her hand. She was always watching my calories and cholesterol. Now, it seems I don't have much of an appetite for anything. I'm sorry to be babbling on, but I'm having a hard time with this . . . being alone."

"That's okay," said Rhonda. "I miss my dad every day. I think I know that feeling of emptiness that you must be experiencing. How about something to drink?"

"A beer would be great if you have one. If not, anything wet will be fine."

"Coming right up. Have a seat. I'll be right back."

Rhonda returned carrying a beer for Garth and a glass of chardonnay for herself.

"What have you been up to today?" he asked while pouring his beer into his frosted mug. "You sounded stressed out earlier when you called!"

"Listen to this. I drove past the J-3 Mission today and saw Sarah talking to a goon who fits the description of the guy I saw following me. It turns out he also drives a black Lexus."

"Damn it, Rhonda. I told you not to take any chances," Garth exclaimed. "Why in the hell would you go near that place?"

"Whoa, wait a minute. He couldn't see me. He wouldn't know my new car. Besides, no one can see through those tinted windows." Rhonda continued to fill him in on all the details—about following John and Sarah and the close encounter at the mall.

When she told him about nearly running out of gas, he said, "Rhonda what in the hell were you thinking? Why would you put yourself in that situation?" His lecture, mixed with anger and concern, brought back memories of her dad.

As he listened, he grew more agitated by the minute. "I don't know what's going on yet, but you can bet he's the son of a bitch that killed your cat and then tried to kill me and killed Susan instead. God forgive me, but if I find him, he will never go to trial. That scum-sucking bastard will die a slow, painful death. That

I promise you." The look in his eyes at that moment reflected more anger and hate than Rhonda had ever seen.

Garth was silent after that outburst, trying to hold his temper and emotions in check. Then he said, "Rhonda, please forgive my unprofessional outburst."

"It's okay, Garth. My sentiments exactly."

"Now," he continued, "please promise me you won't go off like that again. Call me before you do anything. No matter what time it is, call me."

"I promise, I'll call you," she said.

"Good," he answered. "Now, while you were off playing detective today, I did a little sleuthing myself. I spoke to Pablo. He and Moses are going to meet with me in my office tomorrow at nine thirty. I'd like you to be there."

"Okay, I'll be there." Smiling she said, "I'm anxious to see that right-wing capitalist Pablo again."

"Don't drive your car. Take Uber. I'll have a patrolman take you home afterward. I just don't want anyone to get a make on that new car of yours."

"I appreciate the offer, Captain. But I have some stops to make on the way home, so I'll just take an Uber both ways."

"Okay. Before I go, there's something I have to say."

"What's that?"

Garth seemed to have trouble expressing his feelings. "Well, if I had listened to you the first day you came to my office . . . if we had paid attention to Pablo when he reported his friends missing . . . well, maybe things would be different now. Maybe Susan would be home with me tonight." He bit his lower lip and stared at the ceiling in frustration.

Rhonda put her arms around him and laid her head on his chest. "My dad always said, when ifs and buts become candy and nuts, it will be Christmas every day."

Garth gave her a warm smile and a quick squeeze. "Your dad was a smart man. I'll see you tomorrow, little girl," he said as he opened the door and walked off without looking back.

***

Pablo was walking back to Ace Custom Vans looking forward to his meeting tomorrow morning with Captain Kruger, Rhonda, and Moses at the precinct. Walking past the used car lot, loaded with clean used cars, he couldn't resist the urge to check it out. He stood there reading the prices and the comments that were painted in yellow on the windshields—transportation special, $799; cream puff, $1,299; and low mileage, $1,579. He'd cupped both hands around his eyes next to the driver's window of a white Impala, straining to see the interior, when he heard a noise behind him and turned around and came eye to eye with a police officer.

"Freeze," the cop yelled, holding a semiautomatic aimed at Pablo's chest. "Put your hands on top of the car and spread your feet."

Pablo did as ordered. He felt the cuffs snap shut on his right wrist and his arm pulled roughly down behind him, followed by his left arm.

"What's this all about officer?" Pablo protested.

"You're under arrest," barked the cop.

"What's the charge?"

"You'll find out soon enough."

"Ain't you gonna read me my rights?" asked Pablo.

"Yeah, you've got the right to shut the fuck up or I got the right to bust your fuckin' skull if you don't!"

Pablo knew this cop was serious and said nothing more. The cop pushed him into the police van but not before Pablo noticed the NYPD and other markings were magnetic signs that could be quickly applied to convert a regular van into an official-looking vehicle.

After several minutes, he realized they were cruising around making indiscriminate turns— up one street and down another; stop for a few minutes and then move on again. He could see the two fake cops talking up front but couldn't make out what they were saying because of the glass partition separating him from them.

They came to a final stop, and Pablo heard both front doors slam shut. He heard a female voice screaming. The van door slid open, and he recognized the woman as Billy's little friend Willy from the mission. She cowered in the far corner of the vehicle with a look of sheer terror in her eyes screaming, "Billy, Billy, help me." The van sped off into the night.

Some time later, the vehicle came to a stop. Pablo was taken out and escorted into a building he'd never seen before. The officer ushered him into a room that looked nothing like any jail cell Pablo had ever seen. The cop removed the cuffs and, as he was leaving, said, "Have a seat on the couch. Someone will be here shortly to explain your charges."

Now, here he sat, in this strange place. It was clean, comfortable, and warm. But nonetheless, there was no doubt in his mind; he was a prisoner. He looked around for the possibility of escape and saw no windows, no removable ceiling tiles. One steel door locked from the outside. There were surveillance cameras and God knows what else. He knew his only hope was that Rhonda cared enough to come looking for him but admitted to himself the chances of her finding him were slim to none.

***

Pablo had not slept since his abduction last night. He sat on the sofa looking around the little apartment where he was being held. They called it an arrest, but he knew better. Listening to the orientation speech, he'd nodded when told about the court-appointed lawyer who would be in to see him soon.

He wondered about the meeting with Captain Kruger. Had Moses ever shown up? *Are they looking for me now? Or did they write me off as another irresponsible street bum?* He thought about Rhonda. She knew about his future plan and his savings account. She had to know that something bad had happened. She would make the police understand.

***

Rhonda tipped the Uber driver and then hurried into the precinct, knowing she was fifteen minutes late. Garth was at his desk doing paperwork when she came through the door. He smiled and rose to help her with her coat.

"How about coffee?" he said while putting her coat in the closet. He had a decanter of coffee on the side table and a large tray containing danish pastries and doughnuts next to the Weight Watchers coffee creamer.

"How thoughtful," she said as she poured herself a cup and looked up just as Moses came in, almost filling the doorway.

"Is this Captain Kruger's office?" he asked without the bravado he had displayed the first day Rhonda had met him.

Garth turned around and extended his hand. "You must be Moses."

Moses, after a brief hesitation, returned the handshake. "This is the first time I ever been to a po-leese station on purpose. I'm a little nervous."

"No need to be nervous. Help yourself," said Garth as he gestured toward the table.

"Don't mind if I do. I ain't had no vittles since yesterday noon at J-3. Then I had to listen to the Sermon on the Mount from that muthafuckin' motormouth Saint Sarah."

"Well, I don't know about the saint part," Rhonda said with a tone of righteous indignation. "Where is Pablo? I thought you were coming together?"

"I don't know, man. The dude was all excited 'bout me meetin' him this morning. Said you was gonna find out 'bout Levi and Jimmy. I waited long as I could. Then I figured he went on ahead. So I just came over my own damn self."

Rhonda and Garth exchanged glances.

"It's not like him," said Rhonda. "I don't feel good about this. He wouldn't just not show up. I know he wouldn't miss this meeting. Something has happened to him. I just know it."

"I'll tell you one damn thing," Moses chimed in. "When that dude tells you somethin', you can take it to the bank, and he told me he'd meet me. If you ask me, some muthafucka snatched him jes like Levi and Jimmy."

Garth held up both hands in a stopping gesture. "Wait a minute. Wait a doggone minute. It's no time to panic. He's only an hour late. Let's not jump to conclusions."

"I know," Rhonda argued, "but he would have called me. He's responsible—not your everyday homeless vagrant."

"What in a hell is that s'posed to mean?" Moses snorted, his anger beginning to rise.

"I'm sorry, Moses. I didn't mean it like that. I'm just scared and—"

"Okay, both of you calm down," Garth said. "Here's what we're going to do." They both stopped talking and looked at him as though he was going to wave a magic wand and fix everything. "Moses and I are going to go over to J-3 to see if Pablo was there today. Then we'll check out that area near the library."

"Wait," Rhonda interrupted. "We can call him, or at least call for him. He lives in a van at a place called Ace Custom Vans."

Garth reached for his phone, googled, and then dialed Ace Custom Vans. "Hello. This is Captain Kruger, NYPD. We're looking for a Mr. Gonzalez, Pablo Gonzalez. No, he's not wanted for anything. We just want to locate him for a friend. You're sure?" Garth remained silent, listening and nodding his head. "If you see or hear from him, please ask him to call Captain Kruger."

After hanging up the phone, he sat motionless for a moment. "It doesn't look good. It appears he didn't return to his place last night.

"Moses," Garth said, handing him his business card, "go back to the mission. Ask around. See if anybody has seen or heard from him. If you learn anything, call me at the number on the card. But don't call from the mission. We don't want anyone listening."

"Shit, man," answered Moses indignantly. "I've got my own damn phone, one of them free phones from Uncle Sam." With that, Moses said, "I'm on my way."

After Moses left, Garth poured himself another coffee, sat back down in his chair, and said to Rhonda, "I'm going to pay a visit to Ace Custom Vans to see what I can find. Maybe something will show up on their surveillance system."

Rhonda looked at Garth and asked him, "What should I do?"

Garth sternly looked at her and said, "Go home. Don't even think about going near the mission."

"Gotcha, Captain," she said, giving him a

mock salute. "I'll stay in touch." She ordered an Uber as she walked to the main lobby to wait.

Chapter 11

Rhonda woke up early and couldn't get back to sleep. It was only six thirty. She made a cup of coffee and ate oatmeal with blueberries for breakfast. As she sat eating, she would stop occasionally and add some notes to the outline for her article. She was feeling very confident in her upcoming story. Her work was interrupted by the doorbell.

Who could that be? she wondered. She got up to answer the door and looked through the peephole. There were two uniformed officers from NYPD. She opened the door.

"Good morning, officers. What brings you here this morning?"

"You must be Rhonda," said the tall good-looking cop.

"Yes, I am," she answered.

"Well, Captain Kruger asked us to pick you up and meet him at the precinct."

"What's it about?" she asked.

"I don't really know. He said something about breaking news and mug shots of some home-less people."

"Sounds interesting," Rhonda said.   She grabbed her purse and said, "Let's go."

The short officer held the cruiser's back door open, allowing her to get in. As she was fasten-ing her seat belt, the officer quickly pressed the chloroform cloth to her face. They bound and gagged her, laying her down on the back seat of the cruiser.

***

Rhonda woke up on a couch and found her-self in a room she had never seen. She felt very groggy, and the last thing she remembered was getting in a car with two police officers. She tried standing and realized her legs were too weak. She sat back on the couch and noticed a surveillance camera mounted in the upper corner of the ceiling. *I'm being watched*, she realized. She slowly got up and made her way to the door, finding it locked. The place she was being held in appeared to resemble a studio apartment. However, there were no windows. Her mind was racing, while at the same time, she felt sick to her stomach. Looking around the room, all she could think of was, *Where am I? What can I do?* There was no phone, no computer, and no one to ask even. *My phone*, she thought. *Where's my phone?*

A voice came over the intercom, "Take your seat, Ms. Rhodes."

The door opened and a middle-aged man in green surgical scrubs walked in and sat on the chair across from her.

Before he could begin to speak, Rhonda blurted out, "Where am I? Why am I here? What's going on?"

The man smiled. "I cannot say. I'm only here to give you the rules of your stay."

Rhonda found it difficult to sit still and listen, as the rage started building up inside her. She jumped up and began pacing around the small room.

"Sit back down," the man said firmly, "or you will be sedated. I'm going to leave you with this packet, which will explain what is expected of you while you are here in this facility."

The man stood up and walked out. She heard the door lock behind him. She sat in stunned silence, feeling sheer terror and knowing that she was totally helpless.

***

Garth called Rhonda several times that morning to ask her a question about Sarah Barnes and the J-3 Mission. There was no answer on her cell, so he left her a message. He hoped she had just gone shopping or something else nonthreatening. He didn't even consider that she was out investigating on her own again.

After lunch, he tried calling her again. Still no answer. Thinking she may have gone to her office, he called the *City Voice* and asked to speak with Jim Stephens, the senior editor.

"Hi, Jim. This is Garth Kruger, Seventy-First Precinct. I've been trying to reach Rhonda today. Is she there in her office?"

"Good afternoon, Captain Kruger," Jim answered. "I'm glad you called. We haven't heard from her today, which is highly unusual for her. When we didn't hear from her this morning, we were concerned enough that we called her mother. Her mom hasn't spoken with her either."

"Thank you, Jim," Garth said. "I hope there is nothing to worry about, but I'll go to her apartment and check things out personally. This missing homeless person situation is serious enough that I am very concerned. I'll let you know what I find out."

Garth left the precinct and drove to Rhonda's apartment. He found the door locked securely. The manager let him in. He looked around and read her uncompleted article on her computer— it seemed as if she had stopped in midsentence. Dishes were on the table with remnants of her breakfast nearly finished. The large purse she usually carried was not in the apartment. Nor did he find her cell phone. Only one thing was on the kitchen counter—her car keys. The apartment was neat, with no sign of a struggle. It appeared that, wherever she was, she had left voluntarily.

As Garth began piecing together all the facts he had learned up to this point, things kept coming back to that street mission they call J-3. It was time he checked them out.

***

The night was black as ink—no light from the moon, not a single star in the sky. Garth parked a block from the mission and continued on foot. He was not exactly sure what he expected to find, but he was certain some pieces of the puzzle would be found here. The street was deserted, not a soul in sight. He withdrew his lock pick as he neared the building and hoped he still had the magic touch and the lock wasn't too complicated. As he approached the door, he saw some movement out of the corner of his eye. Looking to his right, he couldn't believe his luck. It was a curtain flopping in the breeze from a window someone had carelessly left open.

Garth climbed through the window, closing and locking it behind him. He systematically went from room to room closing the shades. Only then did he feel safe to use the flashlight on his phone. He came to a locked door upon which was written "Mission Directors." He pulled a credit card from his wallet and slid it between the door and the frame with one motion, and the door opened.

Garth stood in the doorway and scanned the office with his flashlight. A huge oak veneered desk—obviously a donation—monopolized the room. A mismatched credenza behind the desk held a telephone and old-style Rolodex. On the back wall was a velveteen painting of the Last Supper.

To the right stood a four-drawer file cabinet painted olive drab. Along the entire left wall were shelves crudely built with iron pipes and plywood. The shelves contained boxes of donated clothing marked male and female, as well as the sizes. There was an assortment of cleaning supplies, tools, and several large restaurant-sized cans of food.

Garth opened the top file drawer. Filed alphabetically were organizations, along with their donations of the past year. All Saints Catholic Church was the first file. In the file were copies of receipts for assorted clothing, slips notating donations of food left over from various weddings, and cash contributions given at Thanksgiving and Christmas. The file cabinet also contained records of gifts from private citizens, other churches, fraternal clubs, and corporations such as supermarket and clothing chains. The second cabinet contained more of the same, including carpenters, electricians, and plumbers who had donated their services free of charge to the mission.

He walked around the desk and sat down in the big brown leather chair that, in the distant past, could have adorned a fine uptown office. He pulled open the middle drawer and found a variety of junk. The assortment included a plastic paperweight with "Jesus Loves You" engraved on it, paper clips, notepads, and a deck of cards with biblical characters on one side and Bible verses on the other—probably part of some kind of religious board game. Garth pulled at the large drawer on the lower right side of the desk. It was locked.

He again reached into his pocket for his lock pick. After he'd applied a little pressure, the drawer slid open. Holding his phone with one hand, he shined the light into the drawer and began thumbing through the folders.

"Pay dirt," he said to himself as he saw folders labeled donors with names.

"Adler, Richard" was the first. The name didn't ring a bell. Nor did Baker, Rudy, or Cates, Tim. He continued on and froze when he came across the next folder—Gonzalez, Pablo. The paperwork contained Pablo's blood type, along with his age, height, weight, and general health.

This isn't any big deal, he thought, until he saw it contained a full DNA profile. "Why" he questioned, "would they need this?" He also discovered, to his dismay, that it contained the location of Pablo's van, as well as the routes he would take home from the mission. Taped inside the file jacket was a recent picture of Pablo.

Before closing the drawer, he picked up the

last folder, only to see that it was labeled "Wheeler, Eddie." He continued to look through the folders he had pulled out and stacked on the desk. He looked for the name *Levi* and found it under Lardell. There was only one Jimmy, last name Stokes. The location for him was Culvert City.

"Oh my God," Garth whispered to himself. "They're all here. All the missing people are named right here." This proved that the mission was involved with the disappearances, but the big puzzle, he thought, was why.

Garth took the files on Wheeler and Gonzalez to use as probable cause for a search warrant. He decided to copy the files and return the originals back to the desk drawer. He didn't want to give away the fact that he had been here. He placed the pages in the copier tray, reaching to push the button.

"Bad idea," came a chilling voice from out of the darkness as the lights were switched on.

Garth looked up into the eyes of a tall dark bald man holding a semiautomatic pistol.

The Magician's coal-black eyes burned like lasers through Garth. "Don't even think of movin', asshole," he said. "Ya just couldn't mind your own fuckin' business. Ya just couldn't leave well enough alone. Everything was going along fine, like clockwork. Then you and that bitch from the paper piss on the parade."

"What do the homeless get out of it?" Garth asked.

"I don't know. I'm not part of that program. My job is to clean up shit ... like you. But it don't make no difference now anyway, because you're done getting in the way.

"What I want you to do now, Captain, is slowly take off your suit coat and throw it on the desk."

Garth did as he was told.

"Now both hands on the wall. You cops know the routine."

Garth felt the big man's weapon press into his back while he took Garth's Glock 17.

Suddenly, a scream came from the back door. "Help me, please! I can't find Willy." Billy was pounding on the door in a state of hysteria.

The Magician glanced toward the back door. In a split second, Garth spun around, swinging his right arm in a backhand motion and catching the big man flush on the temple, stunning him long enough for Garth to deliver a knockout punch.

Garth picked up the man's weapon and removed the cartridges and reholstered his own Glock 17. He propped the man against a vertical pole that supported the supply shelves and cuffed him to the shelving.

Garth quickly went to the back door.   He recognized Billy from Rhonda's description.

"Billy," said Garth, "what are you doing here?"

Billy looked at Garth with pleading eyes. "The policeman took Willy away!"

"Don't worry. We'll find her." He walked with Billy to a small office. "Stay here till I return."

Garth went back to the Magician, pulled up a folding chair, and waited for him to regain consciousness.

The hit man slowly woke up, looking at Garth with a glazed look. Garth punched the Record button on his cell phone and then placed the muzzle of the semiautomatic against the Magician's temple.

"You like games, scumbag," Garth said, pressing the gun even harder. "What's your first, middle, and last name?"

The man stared back with defiance and said nothing.

"This is a form of Russian Roulette," Garth

said as he pulled back the slide while the barrel was still against the Magician's temple.

The Magician stiffened at the chilling sound. The man's eyes displayed the same terror that all cowards show when the situation is reversed. He had seen the look a hundred times before. Garth pulled the slide back one more time.

"Michael Vincent Randazzo. I'm known as the Magician because I make people disappear," he said, now hyperventilating and sweating like a pig.

Garth was familiar with the Magician's reputation as a hit man. He'd been arrested several times for some of the most gruesome murders Garth had encountered, often decapitating his victims; but police could never get a conviction. Witnesses either disappeared or got a serious case of amnesia before the case went to trial.

"Where are the missing people?" Garth asked.

"Hamilton Military Base," he said before Garth could pull the trigger.

"Why were they kidnapped?"

"I don't know. I can only tell you what I know."

"Where is Rhonda Wells?"

"You mean that nosey bitch from the paper?"

"Yes."

"As far as I know, she's hiding in her apartment."

"Who is your boss? And what is his contact number?"

"I don't know his name. It's kept secret. I only know him as Boss."

After hearing enough, Garth picked up the phone and called the precinct for a squad car.

Garth removed the handcuffs from Randazzo's left wrist and pulled him to his feet. "Time to go. Your ride's on the way."

Suddenly the Magician produced a double-edged switch blade from what seemed like out of nowhere. He took a vicious swipe at Garth, missing his throat by inches. However, when Garth threw up his left arm in defense, he felt the blade cut into his forearm and the blood run down his arm. He retreated backward, falling over the chair. The Magician lunged forward, the blade flashing before Garth's eyes. Garth rolled away just in time, drawing his weapon. The hit man raised the knife one more time. But the move came a split second too late for him, as a single shot propelled him backward against the wall. He slowly slid to the floor, eyes rolled back into his head and blood flowing from his chest.

Garth kneeled down next to the Magician, checking for a pulse. There was none. Michael Vincent Randazzo would never kill again.

Garth grabbed a white T-shirt from a donation box and wrapped it around his arm to stop the bleeding. He was relieved that the wound wasn't as serious as he'd thought. He heard the sirens approaching the mission and met the officers at the door.

"Squad car is ready, Captain," said one of the responding officers.

"What we need right now is a coroner. He's dead."

Garth directed one of the deputies to take Billy into the precinct for questioning.

After the body was taken away, with the squad car following, Garth stood alone. Picking up the chair he'd fallen over, he spotted a cell phone the killer had dropped in the scuffle. He brought up the contact list. There were only three contacts, one of which was "Boss." Garth called the number.

"Yeah, magic man. What is it?" said the voice.

Garth shook his head in disgust and disconnected. He checked Google and drove to the nearest walk-in clinic to get his arm stitched. Despite the late hour, realizing the clock was ticking, he went back to his office to plan a possible rescue at Hamilton Military Base. He knew many lives were at stake. He felt certain one of those in danger could be Rhonda.

Chapter 12

In his office, Garth sat preparing a list of highly qualified officers to make up the elite team to conduct "Operation Street People." His list consisted of seven handpicked men. All of them possessed unique talents, the most important of which was loyalty. The men were seated around a mahogany conference table inside the precinct. They knew this would be something big, as the hour was nine o'clock at night, and every precaution was taken to keep the operation top secret. Garth ordered the room electronically scanned to be sure it wasn't bugged. Operation Street People had to be flawless; swift; and, above all, without warning. Garth felt that, since Hamilton Military Base was now under civilian control and in his precinct, it was his problem to deal with.

"Gentlemen," Garth directed the group while standing at the head of the table holding the remote to the overhead projector. "If we had a month to prepare for this operation, it would be difficult. The fact is, we have less than twenty-four hours.

"As you know, Hamilton Military Base was shut down six years ago in a downsizing move by the government. Some politician or politicians convinced Uncle Sam to fund an HIV research project to the tune of fifty million tax dollars. The boys inside the beltway really believe that the people working in the medical and surgical building at Hamilton actually give a damn about finding a cure for HIV. I believe there could be as many as sixteen people being held there against their will. For what reason? We don't yet know."

Garth looked around the room, processing the varied expressions on his men's faces. "Now you can understand why timing is so critical. It could mean life or death.

"Gentlemen, getting inside the base will be our first challenge. The big challenge will be to enter the medical and surgical building."

Garth dimmed the lights, and all eyes were centered on the first slide. "This is an aerial view of the base." He picked up a laser pointer and approached the screen. "The building to the right is their headquarters. On the north side of the base, right here, is the airstrip running east and west the full length of the property. Here on the southeast corner is our target, the medical and surgical building."

Garth continued to focus his pointer on the medical and surgical building, saying nothing more, while he let the message sink in. "We have been fortunate to locate a former private first class who was stationed at the base. His name is Ken Sumner. He worked at the medical and surgical building and claims to know every inch of the facility. I hope, for everybody's sake, he has a good memory."

Garth moved on to another slide. "This is a drawing provided by Mr. Sumner. You'll notice by the elevation drawing that the building has two stories above ground and two below. While the building was operated by the government, the two above-ground levels were patient rooms. The first belowground level housed operating rooms, physical therapy, and radiology. The extreme lower level contained the heating and air-conditioning systems, storage areas, and the morgue."

Garth brought up the next slide showing the floor plans of each level. "I don't know how much help these will be, since a lot could have changed over the years. We can only assume for now that they are fairly accurate."

"Now, let's consider our options for penetrating the base and the M&S building."

Gary Kerbo, an eight-year veteran with the NYPD, raised his hand. Gary had served three tours of duty with the Navy SEALs and had over a hundred night jumps to his credit. "Captain, what about dropping in?"

"That gets you on the base, but it still doesn't get you into the M&S building. Let's keep that option open."

He looked at Dick Thurmond, another member of the team with Navy SEAL experience. "What do you think, Dick?"

"Well, with two of us on the base, we could at least create a diversion."

Bill Macky raised his hand. Bill was 130 pounds at best, but he was proficient in the martial arts. His nick name was Mongoose because of his wiry quickness. "Captain, can we see the aerial view once again?"

"Of course," answered Garth as he clicked on the Reverse button.

"Captain, you say the fence surrounding the base is charged with high voltage, and the buildings are equipped with infrared sensors, right?"

"That's correct, Bill. Mr. Sumner referred to that as the pump house. They pump fresh air into the sublevels of the M&S building. The vertical shaft goes down eighteen feet, with horizontal pipes going into the two lower levels. The vertical shaft is thirty-six inches in diameter, but the pipes going into the building are only eighteen inches in diameter, too small for a man to crawl through."

"Too small for the average man," Bill Macky said with a grin, "but not too narrow for the Mongoose."

Everybody in the room looked at Garth.

"That just might work," he said with hesitation. "But I'm thinking that the pipes would be screened off to keep out small critters."

"Yeah, but this critter will be carrying hacksaw blades and a side cutter," Bill answered.

Garth paused, running scenarios through his mind.

"Okay, let's try this on for size. We drop Gary and Dick in by parachute, while Bill enters the air shaft. We'll communicate with secure radios. Gary and Dick will deliberately trip the alarm system as a distraction to draw attention to the outside. Bill will enter the lower level to shut down the electrical system. The control panel is here in the northwest corner." Garth again switched back to the floor plan and pointed to the area where the breaker switches were located.

"Bill, if all goes as planned, you will come in through the air duct here in the southeast corner. That leaves five of us. When the juice goes off, Jim Harris and Don Jacobsen will cut through the fence and enter from the southwest corner, while Ron Mercer, Dan Kaiser, and I will repel down to the roof from the police chopper.

"In effect, we will attack from all directions, including from above and below. Are there any more questions?"

Everyone around the table was silent. Each was running the plan through his mind. After a moment, all had nodded in agreement. The general consensus was that this was a workable plan.

"I want each of you to take one of these en- velopes containing pictures of the base and surrounding area, as well as the drawings of all buildings complete with floor plans. Study them. Commit them to memory as much as possible. If you think of anything further, don't hesitate to call me. It's now 3:00 a.m., so go home, get some sleep, and plan to meet here at 8:00 p.m. You'll need your energy!"

With that, the team members gathered their materials and filed out.

***

At eight o'clock, the team met for an hour to go over the plan one more time. Each officer was issued a flashlight, a bulletproof vest, a gas mask, a walkie-talkie, pepper spray, and a stun gun. Weapons such as hand guns or knives were left to personal preference. Bill Macky carried a pistol grip hacksaw, side cutters, a miner's helmet with a lamp, and a supply of smoke grenades.

Kerbo and Thurmond carried a large duffel bag containing a machine gun, a thousand rounds of ammunition, and a tear gas launcher. Night jumps with 150 pounds of equipment was standard procedure for both men in year's past, and those jumps had been into more hostile terrain than Hamilton.

The eight men left the precinct in an un-marked van. Five would be dropped out at the Don Thomas Executive Airport, where a Cessna 172 waited for the two parachutists. A police helicopter stood by to deposit Mercer, Kaiser, and Kruger on the roof of the M&S building.

After synchronizing all their watches, Garth gave some final instructions before Macky, Harris, and Jacobsen left for the twenty-minute drive to Hamilton.

***

Pablo woke up relieved that what he had just experienced was a dream but quickly noted he was still in this locked room, which was a real-time nightmare. He hadn't seen his court-appointed attorney after that first visit. When his dinner arrived, he asked the guard to check on the time his lawyer would be in to visit him.

"Funny you should ask, Pablo," replied the guard. "Barry Hirsch called this morning. He said to tell you he would see you soon."

Pablo finished his dinner. He wondered if Rhonda or Captain Kruger were any closer to finding him. He was becoming more discouraged by the day and was beginning to feel hopeless.

***

The two men dressed in green hospital scrubs watched Pablo on the monitor as he approached the refrigerator. They knew he had an insatiable thirst for orange juice. He poured himself a large glass of juice and then settled down on his couch to watch a rerun of a World Cup soccer game. Soccer always made Pablo home-sick for his native Costa Rica. Within minutes, the drug took effect, and Pablo went into a co-matose sleep.

The door of his suite opened, and the two men entered, pushing a gurney. On his chart was written one order—left cornea.

***

Pablo could see the intense white lights above him. He could hear voices but could not make out the words. He seemed to be drifting in space. He sensed people around him. Someone was injecting something into his left arm. He felt like he was in grave danger, but he didn't really care. Then he felt nothing at all.

He woke up in his familiar room, finding a large bandage covering his left eye. He also felt some pain. He vaguely remembered white lights and voices but nothing else. He swung his legs off the bed and walked to the mirror on the wall.

For the first time in his life, he was speech-less.

***

Rhonda's mood shifted between optimistic and totally hopeless. Sitting on the couch in her prison-like room, she replayed in her mind the possible ways she could be found and rescued. She knew her phone had been in her purse, and she wondered if it had been found or if it was being tracked by GPS. She calculated to herself the timing between when she had been abducted and when Garth or her boss would have realized she was missing. She wondered if the surveillance cameras at her apartment showed the two fake cops who kidnapped her. In her memory, she replayed the list of the many missing homeless people and wondered if they were in this same facility. If so, what would be the purpose?

The voice on the intercom said, "Take your seat please."

Rhonda knew the rules. She took her seat. The guard delivered her dinner tray over two hours late. She looked at the plate, not at all hungry, even though it was her favorite— potatoes and meatloaf. She picked up the cup of black coffee and sipped.

Suddenly, the room began to turn. Rhonda dropped the cup to the floor. She could already feel her memory fuzzing around the edges as her world went gray and then black.

She was quickly wheeled to the operating room. The doctors reviewed her chart again. It read, "Complete package." On a stainless-steel cart next to the operating table were four small ice chests.

***

Garth listened to the Cessna pilot over the radio.

"We're over the target, Captain."

Garth looked at his watch; it was 10:05 p.m. "Kerbo and Thurmond can jump any time," Garth answered.

"Good luck. I'm outta here," said the pilot.

Garth keyed his mike. "Macky, are you there?"

"Yes, Captain. I'm about to clip the electrical wires that power that monstrous fan in the pump house, but the blades are taking their sweet time to stop. I'm going to bend one of the blades back so I can enter the shaft. I've looped a rope around the large fan motor, and I'm now at the bottom of the shaft."

Garth heard him say, "Shit. It's pitch-black."

"Captain, this is going to take longer than calculated. The screen is too high for me to reach, so I'm going to have to make a sling with my rope and try to push it in."

Garth looked at his watch, it was ten twenty-six. Macky should be in the tunnel already, and the jumpers were on the ground.

Garth was in the air about three miles west of the base and figured Kerbo and Thurmond should have ditched their chutes and made their way toward the M&S building. He knew the tall grass in that area would offer them suitable cover. They only had two minutes to cross the wide-open area to the tarmac and runway to get to the M&S building. The plan was for them to split up, with Kerbo going to the barracks and Thurmond, to the headquarters building.

Garth's mike came on. It was Kerbo. Garth could hear the ear-shattering whopping sound of the alarm and Kerbo's voice. "Captain, it's hit the fan."

Chapter 13

Garth stood in the door of the chopper, puzzled by the fact that not a single vehicle was visible in the parking lot. How in the hell did they get here? And how many people are in the building?

He keyed the mike on his right lapel. "Move in when possible. The Mongoose is inside. Exercise extreme caution.

"Harris and Jacobsen, secure the ground floor. We'll be on the roof in two minutes."

"Mongoose, are you okay?"

"Nobody down here," Bill Macky answered. "But I'm expecting company near the switch box."

"Kerbo, Thurmond, try to reach the bottom level. Mongoose will need backup."

"We'll take the stairs on the east end."

Now on the roof with Mercer and Kaiser, Garth heard a shot ring out. He keyed his mike, but there was no answer from Macky. There was nothing he could do to help. He waited a few minutes and keyed his mike again.

This time, Macky answered. "Captain, I was having a little problem, but it's worked out now. Had to dodge a bullet and use my smoke grenade. I'm glad you insisted on the gas masks. The bottom level is secure, Captain. Kerbo and Thurmond are with me, also two dead guards."

"Harris here, Cap. The two floors above ground level are also secure and appear to be deserted."

Garth, making a decision at this point, replied, "Bill, turn the power back on. We don't need to be shooting at each other."

"We'll split up and go down the stairs on each end. You three do the same. With any luck, we'll meet in the middle."

Garth was surprised that it was eerie quiet in the building. The team entered the stairways on each end of the building.

"I'll go up on the east end," responded Bill.

"Good luck. I'll see you at the top."

As the men took to the stairs, Garth noticed the only sound was coming from the sixty-cycle hum of the florescent lights.

Garth led the way with his group. He opened the door a crack. There was nobody in sight. He opened it a little wider to look down the long hallway. The terrazzo floor glistened under the fluorescent lights. Not a sound. Not a movement.

Garth stepped out into the hall and saw the door at the far end open. He pulled his gun and then reholstered it when Macky waved his right arm back and forth.

Into his mike, he began giving orders. "Check every room, slowly and carefully."

Halfway down the corridor was a nurses' station. Garth walked behind the large horseshoe counter and began looking for anything that could shed some light on the operation.

"Captain," came a voice over his receiver, "there's life down here."

"Same thing over here," said another team member. "But the door is locked."

Garth walked down the corridor and found virtually all of his men staring at monitors and the lives attached to those monitors.

Garth ran back to the nurses' station and began rummaging through the contents of the desk, looking for some sort of master code list. There was nothing. He switched on the computer screen and waited with anxiety for the screen to illuminate.

He typed "menu" and then hit the Enter key.

Master file inquiries appeared on the screen, followed by a numerical list. Number 3 on the list was "Individual guests."

Garth hit the number 3 and hit Enter.

Words appeared on the screen: "Please enter the first four letters of the guest's last name."

Garth typed "Gonz" and hit Enter. The screen blinked, and the name "Gonzalez, Pablo" appeared, followed by a variety of information— blood type, favorite food, favorite drink. To the right of his name in parentheses was typed "(Suite #9, 3941)." Garth quickly scribbled down the code and hurried to suite 9. On the keypad, he punched in 3941 and turned the knob. The door opened.

He entered and looked into the startled eye of Pablo Gonzalez. Pablo had no words at he stared at Captain Kruger with his one good eye.

"Captain Kruger?" he said in shock.

"Come, Pablo. I'll explain everything later. I need to find Rhonda, if she's here."

He hurried back to the nurses' station and studied the screen. He scrolled back to the menu. Number 6 was marked "Guest status."

Garth entered number 6, and his heart fell to the pit of his stomach when words filled the screen: "Rhonda Wells, operating room #3, east wing. Surgical schedule: Complete package. 10:00 p.m."

"Holy mother of God," Garth said aloud. "They took her to surgery while we were coming in."

Just then came a voice on his receiver. "Captain, you'd better get down here, operating room number three off the east wing."

Garth arrived to find three of his men standing over the operating table under the bright surgical lights looking at a woman lying on her back motionless. It was Rhonda. Garth couldn't look at the table but directed his eyes to his men instead.

In answer to Garth's unspoken question, one of men said, "It's okay, Captain. She's not dead. She's been heavily sedated. We arrived in time."

Garth walked over to the table. His legs nearly buckled as he inched closer, looking down at Rhonda.

"Gary," he instructed, "get on the horn and get some wagons with paramedics and squad cars out here ASAP. Be sure Pablo Gonzalez is transported to the hospital."

Garth looked at Don Jacobsen. "Don, you're the computer guru. Go back to the nurses' station and try to find the codes to all the locked doors."

"Piece of cake, Captain."

Garth said to Kerbo, "Carry on. Make sure every room is checked thoroughly for any sign of life. Be careful. We think the staff left, but there could be some stragglers. I plan to stay here with Rhonda until she wakes up. I want her to see a familiar face. She's gone through enough terror."

Garth was standing there thinking about everything that had transpired tonight when he heard a slight groan. Her eyes opened with a look of terror—until she saw who was there with her. "Captain," she whispered.

Garth took her hand and said, "It's okay, Rhonda. You're safe. It's all over."

"But where am I?"

Garth answered, "Paramedics are on the way. They'll check you out. Once we know you're okay, I will drive you home and explain everything."

While the medics were examining Rhonda, Garth wheeled away the cart containing the four ice chests he didn't want her to see. They were labeled "human heart, human kidney, human liver, and human lung."

He looked up as Macky came into the room.

"Captain, you need to see this."

Garth followed him into the scrub room just off OR 3. The plaque on the door read "surgical supplies." He opened the door and stood there pointing at the inside, saying nothing.

"What?" Garth questioned as he approached the closet.

Instead of medical supplies, he saw stairs going down to an underground passage. He thought to himself, *That explains there being no cars in the parking lot.*

He walked to the bottom of the stairs and then looked up at Macky and said, "I bet you a dollar we'll find a parking area at the other end."

After all the victims who required medical attention were transported to the hospital, the team called the coroner's office to deal with the deceased who were not yet cremated. They came across a small female whose only identification was a small tattooed heart on her arm with an inscription—Billy.

Before the last two squad cars left, Garth looked at the two remaining officers. "I want you two guys to car pool back to the precinct. I need one car to take Ms. Rhodes home."

On the way to Rhonda's apartment, he looked over at Rhonda. She seemed to be in a trance. He reached out and touched her shoulder. "Rhonda, are you okay?"

"No," she cried and completely collapsed, sobbing uncontrollably.

Garth didn't say anything. He felt that, at this moment, words were not necessary. She just needed to cry. He handed her his handkerchief.

Rhonda tried to smile. She looked at Garth and said, "The most beautiful sight I've ever seen was waking up and seeing you standing there."

"I've never been accused of being a beautiful sight, but I was glad I was there."

Garth felt relieved that she was returning to the tough kid he'd come to know. She was much calmer, and the tension lines around her face relaxed.

"Captain, the thing I remember is two uniformed police officers at my door telling me you needed me at the precinct, and there was a big story breaking. I was getting into the back seat of the cruiser, and the next thing I knew, I woke up in that terrible place back there. For the last couple of days, I was locked up in a strange room wondering if I was going to be human trafficked or held for ransom, given that my family is very affluent. I don't know anything else."

Garth answered, "Speaking of family"—he handed her his cell phone—"your mother is frantically waiting for any information. You need to call her right now."

After the call, Garth watched Rhonda disconnect. "How is your mom?" he asked.

"She's relieved and will be here tomorrow night. Captain, can you fill me in on the details of what has been going on and what we can expect going forward?"

"While the news media has already picked up some information regarding our operation here tonight, they don't know half of the details. But you will break the story. I do have some good news that should put your mind at ease."

"Great. I could use any kind of good news after what I've just been through."

"First off, I spoke with Jim at the *City Voice*. He is very happy that you're safe, and he wants you to call him when you feel up to it. Secondly, the detectives pinged your cell phone in the attempt to find you. Instead, they found your cell phone and your purse, which still had your wallet inside, along with credit cards. The last thing these guys needed was anything that could be traced, so they dumped it. Did you have any cash?"

"Yes, but I am so thankful to have my phone and credit cards, I'm not worried about the cash."

"It's locked in my office. So you can pick it up in the morning. Plan on being there at eight o'clock tomorrow morning. We have a lot to document regarding this case. Now, for the best news of all. Remember that guy in the Lexus?"

"How could I ever forget?"

"You never have to look over your shoulder again. We had a confrontation at the J-3 mission. He attacked me with a knife. Long story short, I had no choice but to kill him in self-defense."

Rhonda let out a long sigh of relief. She smiled for the first time in days and said, "Thank God."

They pulled up to the apartment and parked in the guest spot. Garth walked her to the door.

"Rhonda, are you sure you're going to be okay alone here tonight?"

"Absolutely, after knowing that madman is

dead. Would you like to come in and have a coffee or drink before you leave?"

"A drink sounds tempting, but I have a ton of paperwork to do before tomorrow morning. Get a good night's sleep and be prepared to get the news scoop of the century. I'll see you in the morning."

Chapter 14

Garth was awake before sunup. He had difficulty sleeping in that big bed alone. He went to an all-night restaurant called the Country Skillet for breakfast. He was finishing the last of his bacon and hash browns when his cell phone rang. His caller ID showed Wade Newman was the caller.

"Hell of a job last night, big guy. I smell a monster promotion coming up."

Garth's expression was grim, but he tried to cover his loathing and answered in an even tone. "I was just doing my duty, Commissioner. What can I do for you today?"

"Well, for starters, you can be in my office for a nine o'clock press conference. Oh, I know you don't care for the limelight. But by God, you at least ought to show up and take a bow. Like the kids say today, you da man."

"Commissioner—" Garth began.

"Garth, don't you think it's time you start calling me Wade?"

"If you say so . . . Wade."

"Well, I do say so. And it's about time we bury the past and get on with the future."

"Yes, sir. It's time to face the future. I'll see you a few minutes before nine."

***

When Garth arrived at the precinct, Rhonda was already there and waiting.

"It's great to be back on the beat," Rhonda said. "So, what do we do next?"

"What do we do? You and I are going to a news conference upstairs in the big room outside the commissioner's office. I have been summoned."

There were so many reporters at the press conference that they had to move into the large waiting area outside the commissioner's office. Wade Newman arranged to have coffee and pastry available for the members of the media. TV lights and cameras were crowded around a podium containing a couple dozen microphones. The media gathered near the back of the room, ready to make a beeline for their offices in time for the next edition.

"Could I have your attention please," Commissioner Newman stated as he took the podium.

"Look, the asshole is wearing makeup," Garth whispered to Rhonda.

"Ladies and gentlemen, this could turn out to be one of the most bizarre cases in the history of this city, or anywhere for that matter. We have been working on the case for several weeks, which involved an undercover operation by the Seventy-First Precinct—under the direction of Captain Garth Kruger and this office, of course. We have uncovered a mass kidnapping scheme. And although we have not yet made any arrests, the good news is we successfully rescued several people last night at a location that I'm not prepared yet to divulge. I'll now turn this over to Captain Kruger, a man for whom I have the upmost respect. His tireless efforts made the rescue last night possible."

Wade, in his most pompous stance, motioned Garth to come forward and then backed away with his hands behind his back, resembling the commandant in the TV sitcom *Hogan's Heroes*.

Garth approached the podium, straightened his tie, and glanced back at Wade before continuing. "I don't have a prepared statement and will only address last night's rescue. We have uncovered a diabolical scheme, which is the backstory to last night's operation. Several of the persons kidnapped have been brought to the hospital, and the majority of them are members of the homeless community. I'll take your questions at this time. You—in the back."

"Captain, you mentioned a diabolical scheme. Can you elaborate on that?"

"No, but I can tell you that we have substantial evidence, which we gathered last night, that will prove the case. However, I cannot address the details at this time because it would jeopardize the investigation going forward."

Garth paused for a moment and looked at his watch, stalling in an attempt to gather his thoughts. "Rather than having you ask questions that I cannot answer at this time, I can confirm that the scheme involved corruption at many level—"

"Captain," a reporter in the front row interrupted, "what do you mean by many levels?"

"It involved religious charities, the medical community, and even political figures."

"Captain," asked one reporter, "how high up the political ladder are we talking?"

"That's a good question. We may never know how high it goes, but I do know where it begins."

Garth appeared to be carefully framing his next statement. The silence in the room was uncanny; every eye in the room begged him to continue.

"Some members of the NYPD are known to be involved."

Garth glanced over to Wade Newman to see the expression of shocked disbelief on his face.

Wade stepped forward and abruptly snatched the microphone from the stand. "This news conference is over," he said. "Anything that we may say at this time would be speculation. Thank you for coming. Please clear the room."

He then turned to Garth. "I want to see you in my office. Now. We need to discuss strategy."

Before following the commissioner to his office, Garth made eye contact with Rhonda and motioned her forward. "Rhonda, go down to the reception area and wait. This shouldn't take long."

Garth tapped on the commissioner's door and walked in.

The commissioner looked up from his desk and said, "What the fuck were you trying to do out there? Why are you tying this to us?"

"Not us," Garth responded, "you."

"What? You crazy son of a bitch!" His face twisted in an angry sneer. "You crazy lowlife son of a whore. You have no right collecting evidence and then withholding it from me. I'm the commissioner. I'm your fucking superior." He glared at Garth with pure hatred in his eyes. "I always knew you hated me, ever since I was promoted over you. I knew you've been jealous of me for the past six years, but I never thought for a minute that you would stoop to something this low."

Garth remained calm and quiet, allowing him to finish. "It's over, Wade. We found the floor safe in the basement with volumes of documented evidence in the M&S building near the crematorium. I believe the documents found in the safe will stand up. Names, addresses, Swiss bank account numbers—we have it all."

The commissioner stood up; walked around his desk; and, as he grabbed Garth by his lapels, snarled, "I'll have your ass for this, you prick. You'd better have your fuckin' ducks in a row, because your career is about to go down the shitter."

Garth backed away and continued to stare into the wild eyes of Wade Newman. Quietly, he began talking. "It's over, Wade. It's over."

"It's not over till I say it's over. Now get the fuck out of here."

With that, Garth turned and walked out of Wade's office. As he was walking away, he heard the lock click and watched the vertical shade close. He took the elevator down to the first floor. He stepped off the elevator, looked around, and saw Rhonda sitting in the lobby waiting.

"Rhonda, let's go into my office. We have a lot to go over." Garth sat in the chair behind his desk; leaned back; and threw his hat on the credenza behind him, massaging his neck for a moment.

"What a day, Rhonda. What a day."

As Garth was organizing his reports from last night, Rhonda spoke. "You were right about one thing, Captain. That news conference was unforgettable. But it was also uninformative."

"I had no idea the commissioner was going to shut us down. But look at it this way—all the information those reporters missed you're going to get. I believe you've earned it. Just be patient." Garth reached into his file drawer and pulled out a form with the words "Official Police Report" printed across the top. He handed it across the desk to Rhonda. "I want you to take your time. Write everything you can remember about your kidnapping ordeal, including descriptions of the officers who picked you up. Don't leave out hair color, eyes, any detail you can remember no matter how small it may seem. Whatever you saw or heard, write it in the report. While you are doing that, I'm going to finish my reports from last night. But first, I'm going to get a coffee. Can I get you anything?"

She answered, "A bottle of water would be nice."

Before Garth could walk around his desk, they were interrupted by a loud pounding on his door. Garth opened the door to see a young rookie officer with a shocked expression on her face.

"What is it?" Garth asked.

"Sir, a shot rang out upstairs in the commissioner's office. We tried to go in, but the door is locked."

Garth said to the officer, "I'm on my way. Run down to maintenance and bring me a master key. I'll be upstairs." He then said to Rhonda, "Finish your report and wait here." With that, he ran in the direction of the elevator.

Garth cautiously approached the commissioner's office and tried to open the door; even though he knew it was locked, he tried it anyway. He walked into an adjoining office, picked up the phone, and dialed Wade's extension. From outside, he could hear the phone ringing in the office. After the second ring, he hung up.

Just then the young officer, out of breath, ran across the room holding the master key and handed it to Garth.

"Thanks," he responded. "Stand by. I may need backup."

Garth unlocked the door and, with a controlled motion, pushed it open with his foot. He slowly entered the office to find Wade Newman sitting at this desk, facedown in a pool of blood, a gaping hole in his head still oozing. With haste, Garth approached him and placed two fingers on his carotid artery. "He's dead, and I'm afraid a whole lot of valuable evidence died with him."

Garth turned to the officer. "Please keep everybody out of here for now, and get the coroner up here as soon as possible."

Alone with only his dead nemesis as company, Garth dropped into a large chair on the other side of the desk. He leaned back, closed his eyes, and was thankful for the silence.

Before the coroner's arrival, the silence was broken by the sound of a laser printer inside the credenza behind the commissioner's desk. He walked over and opened the door as the printer completed page three of Wade Newman's mea culpa, which began, "God forgive me."

With care, Garth removed the three pages and placed them down on a nearby table for viewing. It read:

God forgive me. I'm waiting for my fellow officers to come for me. I wish I had the courage to face them. Again, I'm taking the easy way out. To Jennifer, Jared, and Jake, I'm sorry for what you will endure because of me. To the victims and their families, I'm sorry. I played God with their lives and yours. Now, I will pay with my own.

To state and federal authorities, the others must also face the consequences of their actions. You must stop them. John and Sarah Barnes were part of the scheme from the start. The blood samples were not for AIDS detection but, rather, for DNA and tissue matching purposes.

Of the eleven doctors who comprised the Beau Monde Society, to my knowledge, they are all dead. The communication devices they were mandated to wear at all times were equipped with a C-4 charge explosive. The devices were detonated simultaneously by one phone call. I personally dialed this number at six thirty this morning when I saw the surgery venue fall to law enforcement.

Lieutenant Governor Gene Wilkins, my father-in-law, was first in command. Not only was he aware, he set up Swiss bank accounts and paid all the bribes. To whom? You will have to ask him yourself.

US Senator Lee F. Paterson, Gene's business partner and former college roommate and once head of the Military Affairs Committee, arranged for the use of Hamilton and suggested the AIDS research grant as a cover.

To Garth Kruger, my constant nemesis, I'm glad it's finally over.

***

Garth waited for the coroner. As they wheeled the commissioner's covered body into the elevator, Garth took the steps down to his office.

Rhonda stood up as he walked into his office and sat down behind his desk. "What's going on? I've been sitting here waiting and fearing the worst."

Garth said, "I thought I'd seen it all. I want to give you this." He handed her a copy of Wade Newman's confession. "I'd say you have your story in your hands right now. This was left by the commissioner before he shot himself in the head thirty minutes ago. All the nasty details are here. Like the great Paul Harvey would say, now you know the rest of the story. Until morning, it's for your eyes only. You get the honor of breaking the story of the century. You'd better get moving. You have a Pulitzer column to write."

She stood there, studying the letter. Then she looked at Garth. A tear escaped and trickled down her cheek, falling to her notepad.

"What is it?"

"Whether it's a prizewinner or not, it will be my last article for the *City Voice*."

"What do you mean last?"

"I'm moving to Florida. I need some peace and quiet. I thought I wanted the excitement of New York. Now I think I have had enough. My mom moved to St. Petersburg, and I miss her. I miss Todd. I sorely miss my dad. And now, moving away, I'm going to miss you, Captain!"

"After what we've been through, why don't

you call me Garth?"

Rhonda's memory flashed back to the nickname her dad had called her. "Okay, Garth, and I wish you would call me Ronnie."

Garth answered, "I'm going to miss you, little girl. Lisa and I talk often about taking Katie and Chipper to Disney World. So now we have an excuse to go."

"I have a lot to write before the deadline. I'll call you later to get your thoughts before it goes to press."

Chapter 15

City Voice

Plight of the Homeless Series

By Rhonda Rhodes, Staff Reporter

As of last night, any article concerning "the plight of the homeless" is but a snippet of what has been uncovered since my last edition. As I write this, I find myself lacking adequate verbiage to describe the diabolical greed, corruption, and inhumanity that have been uncovered. A travesty has been playing out for over three years under the collective noses of the citizens of this great state.

From a nondescript, so-called religious street mission that collected DNA and blood samples of the homeless under the guise of free AIDS testing, there arose a cultic organization called Beau Monde Society. This group believed that eliminating the "unproductive" while saving the "productive elite" who needed lifesaving transplants seemed a noble cause. They called themselves a noble society. Law enforcement calls them a clandestine syndicate. Any human being with a heart would call them the diabolical work of the devil. The customers are the rich and famous, who have neither the time nor the inclination to go on a waiting list. If a celebrity is in need of a heart, liver, or kidney, all he or she has to do is deposit the required sum of money in a Swiss bank account. VoilÃ ! No lines; no waiting.

Sixteen people, including yours truly, were rescued from Hamilton Military Base. How many died we may never know. You may remember that base was shut down due to a government cost-saving measure. But with the help of a few corrupt government officials inside the beltway, it was designated as an AIDS research facility, along with a $5 million taxpayer grant.

Sadly, what went on inside the facility had nothing to do with AIDS research but everything to do with making the rich richer. The society made every effort to sell as many healthy organs from one "donor" as possible before that *person* succumbed to death. The object was to utilize corneas first, followed by a single kidney.

This way, the donor was kept alive until the organization received orders for the heart and liver. There was a crematorium in the lower level where the staff at the facility disposed of the remains.

Their enforcer, who is now deceased, was killed in an altercation with the NYPD. This man was employed by the Beau Monde Society to eliminate anyone who threatened the operation in any way. My recent articles nearly led to my demise, as I was kidnapped, held in a prison-like cell, and slated to be an unwilling organ donor. Documents found that the subject of my first article, Eddie Wheeler, died, and his remains were cremated on-site. Another subject of our series was Pablo Gonzalez. He lost a cornea moments before the raid took place, and thus, his life was spared. Two other homeless men, Levi Lardell and Jimmy Stokes, were found deceased and identified.

It was discovered that Police Commissioner Wade Newman was in charge of the New York City operations. When he saw his house of cards come tumbling down, he took the cowardly way out. He barricaded himself in his office and typed and printed a complete confession, prior to committing suicide. While on the subject of Mr. Newman, it is interesting to note he is the son-in-law of Lieutenant Governor Gene Wilkins—the same Gene Wilkins who is a business partner and former college roommate of US Senator Lee F. Paterson.

There will be more information forthcoming and the *City Voice* will keep you informed when additional facts are gathered.

With mixed emotions, I am announcing that this is my final column for the *City Voice*, maybe for any newspaper. I will be relocating soon to the state of Florida. In closing, I want to thank Captain Garth Kruger for his excellent police work. My sources tell me that he is slated to be the next commissioner. I wish to thank our editorial staff and recognize my late friend and mentor Phillip Brown and all my colleagues. But most of all, I thank you, my loyal readers. Goodbye and God bless.

***

Rhonda completed the article, forwarded it to Garth, and waited for his response.

Five minutes later, his sincere reply came. As she answered her phone, the first thing she heard was, "You did good, kid," in Garth's best Bogart impression. "You've become like one of my own. If there is anything you ever need, you have my number. By the way, Chipper, Katie, and I are looking forward to our trip to Disney World this winter. We'll see you in the Sunshine state."

"I don't want to say goodbye," Rhonda said. "It seems so permanent."

"Don't worry about that. We'll be in touch often."

"You take care. I'm going to need you to walk me down the aisle."

Garth said, "That will be an honor."

"Thank you, Garth. We need to end this call," she said, her voice cracking.

"Good idea, Ronnie. Have a safe trip."

Rhonda leaned back in her chair, fighting back tears. She closed her eyes. A peace came over her. "Tomorrow is a new day," she said to herself. "The nightmare is over."

Epilogue

John 3:16 Mission (J-3 as it was called) was bulldozed. The money seized during Operation Street People was appropriated to build the new Culvert City Drop-In Center. The homeless would now at last have an address and phone number, even though they didn't have a place they could call home.

Eddie Wheeler's ashes were discovered in the basement, along with the ashes of the many missing homeless, near the crematorium. All were interred in the garden at the drop-in center.

Sarah and John Barnes were both sentenced to thirty years in prison for their part in the syndicate. They would be seventy-two and seventy-one when released.

Billy was found dead from an intentional overdose at a "shooting gallery" near Culvert City. They found a scrap of paper in his pocket.

On it, he had scrawled in his childish hand writing, "Plees put my ashes neer Willy. I love her."

The Beau Monde Society was administratively dissolved, as all former members were either found guilty and incarcerated or still under investigation by the New York Attorney General. Some may never be identified.

Dr. Lawrence McGrath supplied valuable information regarding the syndicate. He broke the rules one time by removing his communication device, thereby saving his life. He would live at Attica Correctional Facility for the remainder of his life.

***

Pablo sat in his trailer office at Last Chance Car Company looking out through one eye at his lot filled with ten-year-old vehicles—except for one, his brand-new Ford Expedition. Pablo only bought American. The patch over his left eye, along with a gauche pinky ring, made him look like the used car pirate that he had become. His plans were to someday own a legitimate dealership. Nobody was betting against him.

Rhonda decided to remain in the news media

and was working for the *Ledger* in Lakeland, Florida. She lived on a lake with her tennis pro husband, Todd Scott, and her young son, Garth Kruger Scott. She wrote a daily column called "People, Places, and Things." She stayed very much in the middle of the road—nothing too extreme—as she'd had enough controversy to last a lifetime!

NYPD Commissioner Garth Kruger lived in his house on Crest Drive. He spent a lot of time with his grandkids, while trying to develop a better relationship with his son-in-law. Ben actually went to a Giant's game with him at the Meadow Lands. He coached Chipper's T-ball team and still read the sports page every morning. Before leaving the house, he would pause just for a moment and listen for Susan's voice saying, "Hey, be careful out there."

The city's sixty-three thousand homeless, well, they were just trying to get through the day.

www.ingramcontent.com/pod-product-compliance
Lightning Source LLC
Chambersburg PA
CBHW061146170626
46809CB00003B/997